# THE GIFT OF ENCHANTMENT

"Close your eyes, Elinor!" I said. When she did, I did, too. Then I spoke the words:

> *Rose, rose, red against sky,*
> *Turn into a butterfly!*

I reached deep into myself for the wish to make it so. Rose, I thought, spread your wings of petals and fly! My name is Ceridwen, and I have the power to change you! Rose, Rose! Become a butterfly!

Before I had time to open my eyes, I heard Elinor cry, "Look, Cerri! You did it! Cerri, you did it!"

# LOST MAGIC

Berthe Amoss

Hyperion Paperbacks for Children
New York

First Hyperion Paperback edition: March 1995

1   3   5   7   9   10   8   6   4   2

---

Library of Congress Cataloging-in-Publication Data
Amoss, Berthe.
Lost magic/Berthe Amoss — 1st ed.
p.   cm.
Summary: In the Middle Ages, orphaned Ceridwen learns
the art of herbal healing and gains the protection of the
local lord until she is accused of witchcraft.
ISBN 1-56282-573-9 (trade) — ISBN 0-7868-1034-3 (pbk.)
[1. Orphans — Fiction.   2. Healers — Fiction.
3. Witchcraft — Fiction.   4. Middle Ages — Fiction.]
I. Title.
PZ7.A5177Ln   1993
[Fic] — dc20      93-10082      CIP      AC

For Elizabeth Gordon,
who knew it was there
and dug until she found it
— B.A.

# LOST MAGIC

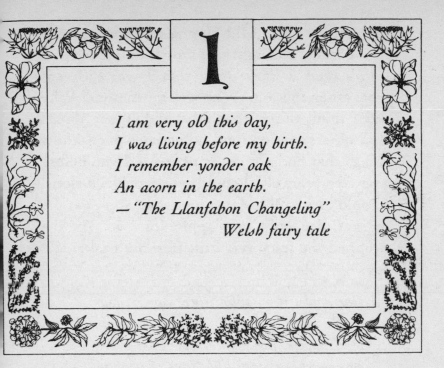

*I am very old this day,
I was living before my birth.
I remember yonder oak
An acorn in the earth.*
— *"The Llanfabon Changeling"
Welsh fairy tale*

OLD HENNE FOUND ME, a half-starved infant, bundled in a basket and floating like Moses amid the flotsam of the moat. Some said that I was a wicked fairy child, for what human mother would set her own infant adrift in such a fashion? But Old Henne, whose hut leaned against the wall and served as a gatehouse, waded out into the mucky water, grabbed the basket, and brought me home with her. She kept me until I turned ten and became an impediment to her boisterous evenings.

I sometimes heard talk that I did not fully

understand when Old Henne's visitors saw me in a corner. I caught the words *changeling* and *witch's child*. I knew only that I was different from other children. Who was my mother? Why did I think things that most didn't, see things that others missed, and sometimes even know things that had not yet happened? Even before I was ten years old, I could create small illusions. I could make Old Mary, who sold apples at the market, see only one apple for two. As she dropped the juicy red fruit into my basket, I'd say:

*One apple, two apples, three apples, four,*
*In the blink of an eye, give me some more!*
*Four apples, five apples, now I have six;*
*I'm watching carefully! None of your tricks!*

But the same illusion failed to fool Old Henne, who'd count the apples one by one when I returned from market. She'd make me stand before her and eye me carefully. "Twelve apples for two pence?" she said once, when I'd eaten an apple on the way home. "I count eleven."

"No, no, Ma Henne, it's twelve. Dame Mary counted them twice herself. Look! One, two —"

"Waif, there are eleven apples here, and you have eaten one. Don't try your foolery on me!"

One evening, the castle cook brought us a tasty pudding. "I can make a pudding like that!" I bragged.

"Is there nothing you can't do?" Old Henne said sarcastically. "You lack the spices to make a pudding, and they are too dear for the likes of us!"

"But I can do it!" I knew I could if I set my mind to it. "Watch me," I said. "Look into my eyes!" I picked up Old Henne's bowl of gray tasteless porridge that was our daily meal and said the words that came into my head:

*Nutmeg, cinnamon, spices rare,*
*Change to pudding our simple fare!*

"Now, taste it!" I commanded. Old Henne's eyes never left mine as she put the spoon to her lips and carefully deposited a bit of porridge on her tongue.

"Lass," she said, "how did you do it? No, don't tell me. Never, never tell what you can do, or sure as I taste this spicy pudding, they will burn you for a witch!"

"But I'm not a witch, Ma Henne! You know that!"

Old Henne finished her pudding, and then she said, not unkindly, "How can I go on keeping you, Waif?" She gestured around the one-

3

room place, which was little more than a hovel. "The folks who come to see me ain't used to watching what they say; they talk rough and use words no child should hear."

"Never mind about that, Dame Henne! I know most of the words now, and I won't listen anymore so I won't learn any new ones. Please! I'm used to here, Old Henne," I added, forgetting to address her with respect. Old Henne treated me kindly when she remembered I was around, and I liked doing as I pleased the rest of the time. "Please let me stay!"

"No, lass, my mind's made up. We'll build you a place not far off, and it'll be for you alone. 'Tis more proper," she added with a nod.

I knew what had made her mind up, and it had nothing to do with what was or wasn't proper. It was changing porridge to pudding that bothered her — that and Mother Barber, the old crone who'd been burned for a witch last Midsummer Eve. They said she'd cast the evil eye on Edith, Harold, and Isaac, who'd been playing near her stall at the marketplace, and when Isaac sickened and died, they'd tried her for a witch. What really happened was that Mother Barber had given us some of her mushrooms in payment for rescuing her cat from atop the stall. Harold and Edith had witnessed against Mother Barber at her trial, but I'd told what was the truth, how the mushrooms were delicious and how Isaac had complained about belly- and headaches the day *before* he'd eaten them. Mother Barber was just naturally cross-eyed and couldn't look any other way but seemingly evil, even when she was being good.

"Waif," Old Henne had said, "how is it that you are always seeing different from what is — from what everybody else sees? It don't make friends to be always expressing contrary ideas to what most say, and it does no good or changes even one person's thinking. Mother Barber was a witch and no mistake. She burned for her evil ways, and it's no good having you sit there in the corner blurting out vexing notions."

So Old Henne undertook to build a separate place for me. She managed to beg two freshly skinned hides from the tanner in exchange for enough ale to thicken his tongue and addle his brain. She rubbed the hides with salt and lime and spread them in the sun until they were dried hard as a board and impervious to water. Together we stretched them between poles so that I had two walls that backed against the castle wall and opened to the banks of the stinking moat. My roof was made of thatched reeds, and my door had once been Old Henne's only rug.

This hovel was my home, with a view across the moat and then the mead, over which my eye could travel along the winding road to the distant village and the forest and hills beyond. On a clear day and an empty stomach, I might sit for hours watching the travelers as they approached the castle gate. I dreamed of the day a handsome couple might ride up to Old Henne, seeking the baby who'd been stolen from them and set adrift in a basket.

I knew, of course, that it was a dream, but it was a dream that just could come true. I never tired of pretending that perhaps this was the day I'd be found, and there, driving that wagon filled with winter apples for the castle, were my parents. I'd carry the dream to a reunion scene, so vivid I'd start to cry, and then realize that it was hunger pains that had brought on the tears.

Occasionally, Old Henne shared her meal with me, but mostly I learned to get my own food wherever I could find it: gathered in the woods or filched from the market stalls when no one was looking or sometimes, on feast days, received as alms from the castle. But I took the warning Old Henne had given me, and I was careful to keep my tricks to myself; I'd learned that people don't like those who are different from themselves.

I never stopped looking for my mother, studying faces for a woman who resembled me. I searched in vain for a fond look or any sign that might mean I belonged to someone. The only head of fire red hair that I came across belonged to a peddler's wife, who, one market day, came riding over the bridge astride a donkey that was carrying her husband's wares as well as herself. I pretended I wanted to buy from her a skein of green thread at a very dear price. But when she spoke, I could not understand the words, so ill pronounced they were, and she scowled in such an ugly way, I had no desire to be kin to her.

I was always hungry and always cold. Although the chill could not penetrate the dried skins, it breathed its way up through the straw that served as my bed, slipping in little tongues around the edges of my walls and between the cracks I tried to seal with a mixture of mud, dung, and grass. As Old Henne said, I needed a layer of fat to hold in the heat, but I was thin, and my thick red hair made me look top heavy, a mop turned upside down.

One evening near twilight, at the beginning of my eleventh year, an old woman cast her long shadow across my threshold and begged for a night's lodging. She had come from a land far to the south, she said, wandering up to the town gate on the day of Our Lady's Assumption. There was no one to take her in, or no one who would for she looked ill, and at the time there were rumors that the Black Death had mounted his bony mare and was galloping across the continent from east to west, seeking a vessel to cross the channel.

Gallena, for so she called herself, offered me in payment for her lodging a small vial of powdered leaf she claimed would make a dying heart beat strong again with youth. Such magic meant little to me, but I took her in out of remembrance of how I'd once been helpless and alone.

Although Gallena had intended to stay only a short while, we suited each other, and she remained with me through the winter. When the weather became mild, it turned out that her bones had only been chilled with cold, and she knew how to cure herself with the herbs that were part of her profession. She was what they called a "wise woman" or an "herbe woman" or sometimes a "wilde woman" because she knew the untamed nature of the woods, as her grandmother had before her. All of her knowledge she shared with me, patiently explaining the use of her little jars and bottles, which she kept in a large apron sewn with many small pockets.

In early spring, on mist-shrouded mornings, I accompanied her deep into the woods, where she showed me how to identify the herbs and then, over the long summer days, how they could be dried and stored.

She taught me wondrous things; how, for instance, the herb hellebore, which we found growing on the banks of the Rushmore, bears a blossom pearly white and blessed by God with the power to drive out evil spirits possessing the mind, but that its root is as black as night and can induce mental or bodily illness, even death. She taught me that angelica fights the Plague and that a mixture of mandrake and henbane will kill pain and cause a person to sleep as though dead. All of this and much more she made me keep in my head, asking me questions into the night when all I wanted was to close my eyes and sleep.

Besides teaching me about herbs, Gallena gave me the most precious possession of all: a name. One night, shortly after her arrival, we were huddled close to the small peat fire in the center of my hovel. She lay among the rags she called her bed, and I was nestled in the soft warm reeds I had dried during the summer for my winter mattress.

I had just told Gallena my short life story.

"Child," she said, "you are wise beyond your years. What are you called?"

"I am called Waif," I replied.

"Waif! That isn't a proper name. Have you no saint's name? No name by which you were baptized?"

"Oh yes! I was baptized Mary after our Lady, and my proper name is Mary of the Moat because I was found and baptized in its water and not in a proper church. But Mary is far too grand a name for the likes of me and Mary of the Moat too long. I prefer to be called Waif for that is what I am."

"And what you'll always be if you have such a low opinion of yourself! There's much in a name, child. You are your name and your name is you, so why not have a good one, one that tells you and the world as well that you are somebody?"

"But I'm not," I said miserably.

"You are what you want to be, and I shall tell you your name. Pull up your shirt!"

"No!" I cried modestly.

"Child, I would only explain the meaning of the birthmark I have seen on your rib. Look at it!"

Embarrassed, I lifted my shirt just far enough

to reveal a small blue cross-mark on my left third rib.

"There now! Your name is Ceridwen, and I will tell you why!" Gallena adjusted her bony frame to her rag bed. "Listen!" Her dark eyes sought mine as she began her story.

"In the long-ago, early morning of the world, before the great creatures of the earth had turned into scattered bones and before people thought they knew everything, there were witches, sorcerers, wizards, and fairies who were all very much alike in that they could do magic things beyond the power of mere mortals.

"Ceridwen was one of the most gifted of these spell-makers, and there was scarcely any enchantment she couldn't accomplish if she set her mind to it. Ceridwen was as beautiful as she was wise, and she lived in a great castle submerged in a lake.

"But even sorcerers have their problems, and Ceridwen's problem was her son, Morfran. There was nothing wrong with Morfran's personality, but it was trapped in the hairy body of an ape, crowned with the face of a monster and a rather small brain. Morfran was so ugly, he was nicknamed All-Hideous.

"Ceridwen, like any mother, loved her child,

and she wanted to give him some special gift to compensate for his unfortunate appearance. She studied long and hard in her book of magic, and finally, at the very end, written backward and upside down so that it could not easily be deciphered, she found what she wanted. It was the receipt for a brew of wisdom.

"It was a tedious receipt, requiring all kinds of difficult-to-find herbs that must be harvested and added to a bubbling cauldron at inconvenient times. For example, the bell-shaped bloom of comfrey could only be plucked when found shining in the light of a full moon, and the root of mandrake must be shaped like a man if it was to have an effect. Oh, it was a difficult enchantment, all right!

"Stir a year and a day, read the receipt, and the first three drops to bubble up and out of the pot will yield one sorcerer.

"Ceridwen sighed. Much as she loved Morfran, she was not willing to stand over a boiling cauldron for a year and a day. She hired an old blind man with nothing better to do, and even he thought it necessary to bring a boy, a common waif named Gwion, to keep him company.

"Now, Gwion wanted more than the dubious privilege of stirring a sorcerer's brew and the companionship of an old man, and so, when the year and a day was up, before Morfran could descend to the dungeon of the palace where the cauldron stood ready to yield its gift, Gwion positioned himself, and it was he who received the first three drops when they sprang from the pot.

"Gwion, in his newfound wisdom, knew that the first thing he must do was run from the wrath of Ceridwen. And that he did—through the labyrinth of tunnels under the castle, up the dark winding stairs, and through the great halls and chambers to the portcullis that sealed the entrance, where, with a long dive into the lake, he turned himself into a silver fish and slithered into the reeds.

"Of course, Ceridwen, gifted sorcerer that she was, could change forms as easily as she could slip into a new dress, and when Gwion felt a touch on his fin and saw a sleek brown otter, he knew immediately that it was Ceridwen. With a mighty surge, he broke the surface of the water in the form of a little bird and soared into the sky.

"Then, high above him, he saw a hawk, its talons sharp and spread, spiraling down at him, and quickly Gwion shrank himself into a tiny grain of wheat and threw himself on the miller's floor, hidden amid millions of other identical kernels of grain.

"Ceridwen turned herself into a small black hen and pecked her way across the grain-strewn floor, beady eyes alert for the one that was Gwion. She hunted and pecked until, at last, cackling triumphantly, she found and swallowed him in one peck.

"Nine months later, Ceridwen gave birth to a baby as beautiful as Morfran was ugly, but for Morfran's sake and her hatred of Gwion, she could not stand the sight of the child. Ceridwen wove a basket of herbs and reeds and placed the baby in it. She launched the little boat into the lake and did not even remain to see if it arrived safely on shore.

"Some say that the basket was found by a peasant who raised the baby as her own and that, now and then down through the ages, a child is born with the gifts that were Ceridwen's.

"The only way to tell for sure that a child is descended from the great sorcerer is to examine the child's third left rib, for when Ceridwen wove the boat-basket, she included woad, the ancient herb used by the first Britons to dye their bodies blue, and this herb rubbed off and marked Ceridwen's child with a small blue cross. The same blue cross is found on all of Ceridwen's descendants.

"And so," finished Gallena, touching my left rib, "your name is Ceridwen. And when you know your name, you will understand your gifts. That is the power in a name." Gallena smiled. "Yes, your name is Ceridwen." Gallena closed her eyes and fell asleep.

"Ceridwen," I thought, watching the fire's shadows dance on the hide over my head. It sounded good. The musical syllables wove themselves into the movement of the shadows. I did not think to ask Gallena how she knew the meaning of the blue cross or what she meant by Ceridwen's gifts.

"Ceridwen," I said again, contentedly. Sorcerer or not, I liked the sound of it.

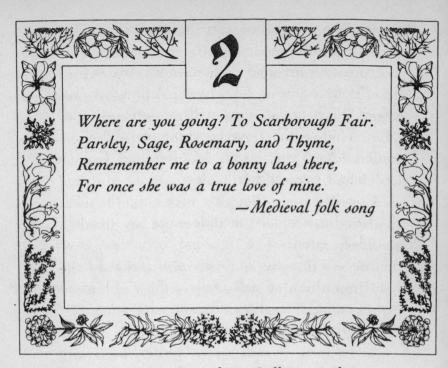

*Where are you going? To Scarborough Fair.*
*Parsley, Sage, Rosemary, and Thyme,*
*Rememember me to a bonny lass there,*
*For once she was a true love of mine.*
*— Medieval folk song*

ONE MARKET DAY, when Gallena and I were trudging along the road over the mead to the village, I started thinking about how much my life had changed since Gallena had come to stay with me almost a year ago.

"Let me carry the table legs," I said to her. We had fashioned a kind of table to show off our herbs at market, a board raised by separate legs made of four straight branches bound into two crosses. Gallena was carrying the board and most of the herbs in a sack on her back.

Before Gallena came, I had spent my days

like the other motherless waifs who lived along the edge of the moat outside the castle wall. I was luckier than most: Old Henne had provided me with a roof and an occasional bowl of porridge. Maybe I spent a lot of time dreaming of a better life, but I did nothing to make my dreams come true; it was enough to survive each day. I had taken Old Henne's advice and had been careful not to let anyone see me at what she called my foolery, which could be mistaken for witchcraft.

Now my days were filled with tasks. In the early hours of the chilly morning, long before daybreak, Gallena would nudge me awake. "Time for breakfast," she'd say, and off we would go to check our traps for a rabbit or dig in the snow-covered earth for a juicy root to stew. In early spring, Gallena showed me how to find the first tender green shoots as they pushed their way up through the warming earth and how to tell the edible mushrooms from the deadly ones.

But Gallena did not consider it enough to cure our hunger pangs. Gallena made me study the herbs. I learned to identify the growing plants, and later back in the hovel, I learned their uses and how to dry and store them. I memorized everything, and long after dark, Gallena tested me until my eyelids grew heavy and my dreams became entangled with my answers.

I tried a trick on Gallena only once.

"Your gifts will amount to nothing without knowledge of how to use them," she said disdainfully. "Making people think they see toads when they are looking at nothing more than stones is just a trick any village witch can learn and serves no good purpose."

It was hard work living with Gallena, but together, we almost made a family and I liked that.

As we trudged along the rutted way, I stole a look at her. Her rugged face was as wrinkled as the road, and I wondered if she had been pretty when she was my age.

I knew that, like me, she had no mother. Gallena's parents had both died when she was an infant, and she had been raised by her grandmother, a wilde woman who understood how to talk to the wild animals and plants that grew about her high in the mountains.

"What was your grandmother like?" I asked, shifting my sack so that I could carry the cross-legs of the table.

"She was different from other people. She spoke very little, only to say do this and do that. She spent her days in the woods with the animals. I saw her talking to them, and one night I saw her dancing in a fairy ring."

"Was she one of them, then?" I asked.

"She may have been. One day, when I was only eight years old, she told me to go down to the village and ask the good nuns at the convent to take me in. She walked out the door and took the path upward. I never saw her again."

I thought about this for a while and wondered if it was more difficult to know and love someone who abandoned you or never to know who might have set you adrift in a leaky boat-basket.

"Hurry!" Gallena said. "I want a stall near the cobbler. My boot needs sewing."

"Did you like the convent?" I asked.

"What? Oh . . . Yes, I liked the convent — for a while. I was put to work in the garden, which supplied the convent with all of its culinary and medicinal needs. Sister Beneface, the gardener, made me work very hard."

"Harder than you make me work?" I asked, only half-joking.

"Much harder. There was so much to be done; it was really three gardens, one for the kitchen, one for the infirmary, and one for beauty. Look! Hurry! There is still a place right next to the cobbler."

We set up our clumsy homemade table, and Gallena balanced the little bottles and baskets on its surface. There was one clear vial, different from the rest, which were made of clay. Gallena took it out of her apron, but quickly put it back in.

"What is that?" I asked.

"It is Monarde," she said. "Nothing important." But the way she said it let me know that it was important; she just didn't want to talk about it.

Gallena changed the subject. "At the convent," she said, "we had a sturdy oak table. There were many small shelves built into it for the jars that we made in our potter's shed. We had everything we needed right there within the convent walls. And we had books." Gallena sighed heavily.

"Did you read the books?" I asked.

"No," she answered shortly. "I didn't know how, and now when I die there will be nothing left of all that I have learned in a lifetime." She looked at me. "Except, of course, what I have taught you that is now in your head."

"Why did you leave the convent then, Gallena?" I asked in between customers, who always bought from us first thing while the herbs were fresh. "Maybe the good nuns could have

20

taught you to read. And the garden sounds like paradise."

"It was," said Gallena shortly. "And I regret that I only learned herb knowledge and did not stay long enough to learn reading. But there was a part of me like my grandmother, a part that was too wild for rigid rules and routine. One day, I walked through the convent gate, and I never went back. Here comes that woman for her lavender!"

We had a regular customer, Dame Woodcock, the wife of a wealthy farmer, who bought all of the dried lavender we could carry to market. She explained to me that she sewed little bags for it and placed them between her linens, bragging that she had a whole chest full of sheets and clothes that she had brought with her when she married.

After Dame Woodcock had made her usual purchase, complaining as always about the price, I showed her a small wreath that I had woven of dried cornflowers, rosemary, and thyme. "It will ward off every disease," I told her proudly, "and looks very pretty besides. I made it. It costs two pence."

"Pride goeth before a fall," she told me, picking at the wreath. "And that is far too dear for such a small bouquet of weeds."

"Then don't buy it," I said rudely, stung by her insult. "Your neighbor, Farmer Mengel's wife, has already bought one just like it."

I heard Gallena draw in her breath at my boldness and the lie that had tripped off my tongue with alarming ease.

"I'll have it after all," said the woman, "if you throw in some fennel for my Ilse's cough."

I burst into delighted laughter the moment she was out of sight.

"Let us hope she does not see Farmer Mengel's wife before you can fashion another wreath and convince Dame Mengel that she needs one like Dame Woodcock's!" Gallena said, and joined me in a good laugh.

Suddenly there was a disturbance. Ma Prigge came running into the square hollering, "My daughter! My daughter! The fairies have stolen her and put a changeling in her place! Help! Oh, please, help me!"

A few women stopped and stared, but none came forward.

"How is it that no one will help Ma Prigge?" Gallena asked the cobbler, who was already repairing her boot in the neighboring stall.

"There's no help for the poor woman," he answered, threading his needle without looking up. "If the fairies have the daughter, she's done for! My brother's child was stolen, and the changeling put in her place does mischief day and night! Why, just last Sunday while my sister-in-law was at church, the little demon unraveled the cloth on her loom — a month's work it was, and — "

"Aye, 'tis true it takes powerful magic to undo the work of fairies," said the cobbler's handsome son, nodding his head wisely.

"But sometimes," said Gallena, "sometimes a human child takes on strange or wild ways and the mother thinks, 'Changeling!' though it is nothing more than a bad case of fires in the body, and those can be quenched with cooling herbs."

"Oh, Gallena," I begged, "try your cooling herbs on Ma Prigge's daughter! I know Edith, and I would give much to see her mended."

"Good, child! This can be your first healing! Let us see if we have made a Wise Woman of you!"

"Me? A Wise Woman? I have no idea what to do!" I cried, dismayed.

"The first thing is to calm down," Gallena said. "The second thing is to examine Edith, and the third thing is to think about what you see and deal with it according to what you have been learning and now know."

Gallena snatched her boot from the cobbler. "Tend our customers, kind sir," she said, moving our table of herbs a little in his direction. She grabbed me by the arm, and we hurried down the narrow street after Ma Prigge.

"Oh, woe!" Ma Prigge was moaning as she waddled around the corner. "There is no help for my Edith! I will never see her again in this world!"

"Ma Prigge! Ma Prigge!" Gallena called after her. "Here is help! Ceridwen knows something of the healing arts, and she is a friend of your Edith's."

Ma Prigge turned as she reached her doorway. "Eh? What say you? That child has healing knowledge?"

I looked down in embarrassment. My mind went blank. I was certainly not going to try any illusions on Ma Prigge, and I couldn't think of a thing that might really help Edith. No doubt Ma Prigge was remembering that I'd taken the opposite side from Edith at Mother Barber's trial. I felt a nudge in my ribs as Gallena shoved me forward, whispering in my ear, "Tell her you wish to see Edith to determine if it is really she or a changeling."

"I . . . I . . . ," I stammered. Another poke in the ribs from Gallena. "If I could see Edith, Ma

Prigge, perhaps I could . . ." A sharp poke. "I'm sure I would know if she was Edith," I finished firmly.

"I can tell you she's not! I know my own Edith. What good can a waif like you do, I'd like to know!"

Ma Prigge's words goaded me. "If Edith is herself, then I will know it, and I can cure her with my herbs," I said, sure of myself at last.

Ma Prigge stared at me critically. I concentrated on trying to look wise, wishing that I had at least combed the tangles out of the curly red mess on top of my head so that my appearance might inspire confidence in my maturity and wisdom.

"Follow me," she said at last. But I didn't need a guide to Edith. Her high-pitched wails were coming from a dark corner in the tiny cottage, where she lay, hands bound, writhing on dirty rags and wrapped in blankets.

"Give her some air!" I said immediately. "Bring her into the light that I may see her!" At least I knew better than to bind her hands and cover her with a hot blanket!

"Edith," I said. "It's me, Waif. Do you know me?"

Gallena grabbed my arm. "Your name is Ceridwen and don't forget it!" she said.

Edith looked at me. "Water!" she croaked. "I'm burning up!" Her face was puffed and flushed; her head thrashed from side to side, slapping her matted hair back and forth against her cheeks. I touched her arm and felt the fire that was burning inside her.

"Unbind her," I yelled at Ma Prigge.

"She'll tear herself to bits!" said the woman. "And there'll be no body left for Edith to return to!"

"This *is* Edith in her own body!" I answered impatiently, loosening the knots myself and throwing back the sweaty blanket.

"Be certain, Ceridwen!" Gallena whispered. "A mistake now and you will pay for it with your life. If she does not recover, they will say you aided the fairies to steal the real Edith, and they will burn you for a witch!"

"I am certain, Gallena," I answered. "Fetch water, please, Ma Prigge, and a clean shirt. Take the oil cloth away from the window. We must bathe her and . . . and boil water for an infusion." I glanced at Gallena to see how I was doing. She looked pleased. "I will cure her, Ma Prigge. This is no changeling; this is Edith."

What had Gallena taught me was best for high fever? Oh yes! Henbane. Boil the soft wooly leaves in vinegar and apply as cool compresses on the forehead and all parts of the body. And lovage — an infusion made of the root in boiling water — will reduce the fever. Later, fennel tea. Fluids — lots of them — to quench the inner flames.

"I can do it, Gallena!" I said. "Have you henbane with you and the root of lovage? Henbane on the outside and lovage inside — right?" I knew it was right. Now I could see the good in the long evenings that had stretched into night when Gallena had made me learn the formulas for healing.

Gallena was nodding her head in agreement and reaching into the pockets of her gathering apron where she kept her cures. "Good, child, you are a beginning Wise Woman, and I leave Edith in your hands. I will go back and tend the stall and then wait for you at home. You must spend the night here."

I felt a moment of panic, but there was so much to do that I didn't have time to worry. I didn't sleep; I worked all night, bathing Edith's hot body, wrapping her in cool damp sheets and changing them as they became hot. I held her head steady and made her sip the tea.

But the fever didn't break, and Edith continued to thrash about, growing weaker before our eyes. Ma Prigge was watching me as carefully as she watched Edith. I could see she believed that she was going to lose Edith one way or another, either to the fairies or to my inept healing arts.

I began to doubt myself. How could I ever have thought that I could handle this alone? I wished with all my heart that Gallena had stayed. The inner sureness of what I was doing disappeared, and I asked myself what she might have done, but I could think of nothing that I hadn't already tried. I attempted to cover up my fears with a swaggering walk and confident manner, but I was not fooling anyone, not even myself.

Suddenly Edith sat bolt upright, her eyes red and wild. She pointed her finger at me and shouted in a strange, unnatural voice, "Save me from that witch! She was Mother Barber's helper!" Then she collapsed in a heap.

I drew back, completely undone. Was this Edith a changeling after all? One look at Ma Prigge told me that I had failed. But how? I'd done everything Gallena had taught me, everything she would have done herself, and I had been absolutely certain that Edith was Edith and no changeling . . . wait! . . . that was it! I had been certain, but I had lost that certainty.

As the night had worn on and Edith hadn't improved, I'd lost faith in myself and my treatment. Hadn't Gallena told me that faith in myself was the most important part of being a Wise Woman?

"If you don't believe, how can you expect anyone else to?" Gallena had said. "You must have faith in what you're doing, or you will not change anything."

Ma Prigge was moving toward me, fury written all over her face. "Get out, Witch-Child!" she said, gripping my arm.

"Wait, Ma Prigge!" I cried and thought the words:

*Henbane and lovage, listen to me!*
*Make Edith well I ask of thee!*

Aloud I said, "Look! Look at Edith!"

Edith was lying on top of her covers, arms spread out and quiet. She had stopped thrashing about and was breathing evenly, a thin layer of sweat beading her smooth brow. The fever had broken, and there was no mistaking that this was Edith, cured and asleep.

"Edith!" Ma Prigge burst into joyous tears. "My child has returned to me!"

By afternoon, Edith still lay sleeping, cool and

dry, and just before I left, she managed a small smile and squeezed my hand. I had cured her! I was a Wise Woman — well, almost — but I *was* learning. On the way home, I had time to think that in all the world there was no one I wanted more to be than Ceridwen, the Wise Woman.

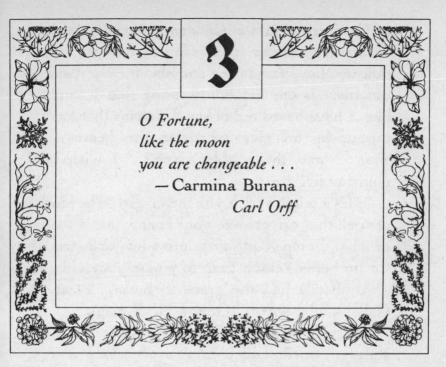

**3**

*O Fortune,*
*like the moon*
*you are changeable . . .*
— Carmina Burana
*Carl Orff*

NEWS OF WHAT I HAD DONE traveled fast. People came to me expecting miracles from the Wise Child-Woman who had brought Edith back from the fairies.

The cobbler's fifteen-year-old son asked me to go with him to his uncle's to rid the family of a changeling and bring back his niece. I would have liked to oblige, for he was very tall and strong with dark hair and he would never have noticed me before, as I was only twelve. When I told him I knew of nothing that could undo the work of fairies, he turned away in disgust.

That night I said to Gallena, "Dame Gallena, I thank you kindly for the knowledge of herbs that you have taught me and also for my name, but there is one more little thing that I would like. I have heard tell of small charms that have the power to give whatever the heart desires . . . and the cobbler's son . . . I wish he might notice me. . . ."

" 'Tis a witch's trick you mean, girl! The kind of spell that can change your enemy into a toad or a handsome young man into a lovesick swine for no better reason than to please yourself."

At that, I had the grace to blush. "Please, Gallena," I begged. "Only a bit of magic."

"Listen to me, Ceridwen!" Gallena said sternly. "Spells and charms are nothing more than tricks with evil at the root and also in the fruit of the deed! There's much good you can do using herbs and someday with the gifts that come with your name, but it must be for a good purpose. You must study to understand your own talents, but don't meddle in the Devil's garden, or as sure as I wag this finger at you, you'll burn at the stake for a witch!"

"But I only mean a small illusion," I said. "I could almost do it myself!"

" 'Tis witchcraft, nevertheless, unnatural and without God's blessing, and that means fire!

Never cross the line, for there's no worse way to die than a burning that continues into hell itself! Nay, Ceridwen, it's a favor I'm doing you not teaching you the black arts. Use your gifts to help others and yourself if your purpose is a good one."

I shivered at her words and looked down at my feet. My toes had grown past the end of the shoes I'd worn when Gallena had first stood at my door, and I'd cut a hole in the tops to give more room. I would soon be starting my thirteenth year, but I was still scrawny and looked too much like Waif and not enough like Ceridwen.

"You are young and impatient," Gallena said, "but I have watched how quickly you learn. You will know what your name really means someday and have everything you seek."

Gallena reached into one of the pockets of her apron and pulled out the mysterious bottle she had called Monarde. "I will give you something better than a puny love potion that any village witch might concoct. This is a powerful enchantment, Ceridwen."

"What'll it do?" I asked in a rude, ungrateful tone.

"First swear by the holy book you will only use it when and if you are desperate."

"I swear!" I said sullenly.

"Ceridwen! Swear by all that's holy!"

"I do so swear!" I said with all the fervor I could.

In the clear glass vial I could see three pearl-like drops no bigger than peas, bouncing about as though they had a life of their own.

"The Monarde is strong fairy magic, child! It is life itself, but its price is death, and that is a riddle I can't answer for you."

"Then you don't even know what it'll do!" I could not imagine any good worth dying for.

As she often did, Gallena answered my question with a story. "One day, when I was still a child, I was walking high in the mountains looking for a bouquet to beautify my grandmother's home. Suddenly I came across a large plant covered with snow-white blossoms. I picked the blooms and carried them home, but when my grandmother saw the lovely flowers, instead of decorating her house with them, she pressed them and extracted the nectar. Then she poured the liquid into this small clear vial, and said:

> *One is for joy,*
> *Two is for sorrow,*
> *Three is for a happy tomorrow.*

"Immediately the nectar formed itself into the three drops you see, and they began their endless dance of life.

"My grandmother told me that she had been looking her whole lifetime for the plant I'd found to make the Monarde. It was a very rare fairy charm, she said, and could only be used once and only in desperate circumstances. When my grandmother walked out the door for the last time, she left the Monarde. I have never known if she meant for me to have it, but I have never needed it, and now it is yours. But remember, you may use it only once, and you must be desperate and ready to die."

I thanked Gallena as graciously as my disappointment allowed and put the Monarde in a corner. If whatever was in the bottle would cost me my life, why would I ever want to use it?

That night as I lay in the dark, not able to sleep, I thought of the blue cross on my rib. What if the mark was meaningless, a mere cluster of blood vessels close to the surface? Gallena had many such marks on her legs. Maybe she had just made up the story about Ceridwen so that I could feel good about myself. I'd have to work and study to understand my special talents, she'd said, but I'd had enough of work and study just learning to be a Wise Woman. What was so evil about working a small charm now and then? Why did it always have to have a worthy purpose?

During the night it grew chilly again, and in the morning frost lay on the land. Gallena awoke shivering and said the cold reminded her that in her southern land old bones could drink the sun all year long and dull vision could be restored with bright light. It was time to leave, she said; besides, there was nothing more she could teach me.

"Leave! Leave me?"

I wanted to tell her that she couldn't just leave me, that she was like a mother to me or at least what I had always imagined a mother might be like, and that I didn't want her to go away. I had expected her to stay always. I opened my mouth several times to say don't go, but the words wouldn't come.

"Will you go back to the convent, Gallena?" I asked finally.

"I have a yearning first to see my grandmother's mountains," she answered, "and then maybe to end my days in the convent, where I can work in my garden once more and — and learn to read."

And what about me, I thought? Wouldn't she

miss me? Didn't she like our life together? Did the convent garden and a few books she couldn't read mean more to her than I did? But she said nothing more, and in the morning she dragged her old body from her bed, packed her things in a bundle, and prepared to take her leave.

"Gallena!" I began, but I was numb with unhappiness and could not say more. She shook her head; her mind was made up. She felt satisfied that I knew as much as she could teach me. She would leave with me all of her herbs, carefully sealed in earthenware vials, and her knowledge of how to use them was already drummed into my young head.

"You have beginning knowledge and wisdom, Ceridwen," she said. "We will have to see what you do with it."

When I was silent, Gallena asked, "Why are you so sullen?"

It should have been easy to say, "Because I love you and don't want you to go." Instead I said, "Because you won't teach me even one little bit of magic."

I didn't even care anymore about the cobbler's stupid son, but it was as though I was under an enchantment that made me say the wrong thing.

"Are you still fretting over that silly spell? Is

that lout worth fire to you? Listen well, Ceridwen! It is for you to discover your own magic, and you will do it more quickly without me. But I can tell you that your gifts go beyond the knowledge of herbs or even the ability to use herbs well."

"How can that be?" I asked. I could not imagine knowledge beyond that of a Wise Woman's or abilities beyond Gallena's — except witchcraft.

"Your name, child! It is a powerful name."

"But maybe you just gave it to me so that I would not be a waif!" I blurted out. Why was it that when I finally found words to speak, they were the wrong ones? But I couldn't stop. "How do I know that you didn't make up the story about what the blue cross on my rib means?"

"Ah! So that is what ails you. Still a lack of faith! But if you lack faith in your name, then you must doubt not only all of my teaching but yourself as well. I will tell you this, although it will not give you faith if you choose to doubt: If ever you are desperate, the Monarde will save you. I am not sure how, because I am only a Wise Woman, but my grandmother knew fairy magic."

"But what could she do that other people

couldn't? Could she change her form like the first Ceridwen?"

"I don't know. I never saw her do so. She may never have wished to, or maybe I did not recognize her in another form." Gallena paused and looked at me hopefully.

I knew she was waiting for me to say something nice, but I was too hurt by her leaving to forgive her, so I said the ugliest words of all, "Well, since no one's used the three drops, who's to say they're magic?"

"Ah, Ceridwen!" was all she answered. "God bless you, child. Some day you'll understand." Again she lingered, but I did not want to let her think that giving me three drops of an enchantment that would kill me if I used it made it all right for her to abandon me.

As she trudged away, down the road away from the castle, I watched her grow smaller and smaller. When I couldn't make out her figure anymore, I went inside and cried. I cried because I had not been able to say to her what was really in my heart, and I cried because I had been abandoned all over again and this time it was much worse.

For days I cried at the least excuse, but gradually, as Christmas approached, I began to feel better. I fell back into the pattern Gallena and I had followed of rising early and working with herbs, and I began to realize that Gallena had not abandoned me in the same way that my own mother must have nor even halfway as Old Henne had. Thanks to Gallena I was on my way to becoming a Wise Woman. Gallena had cared for me and taught me everything she knew. Surely no mother could have done more for me.

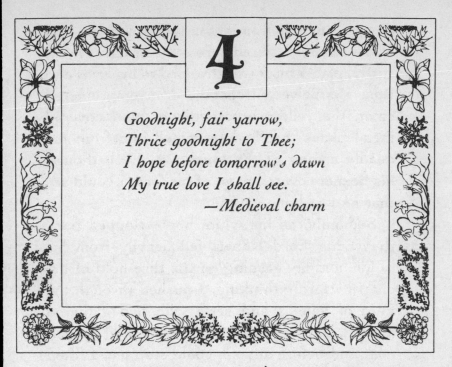

## 4

*Goodnight, fair yarrow,*
*Thrice goodnight to Thee;*
*I hope before tomorrow's dawn*
*My true love I shall see.*
       *— Medieval charm*

NOT LONG AFTER GALLENA'S DEPARTURE, as the season was changing from winter to spring and there was still frost nipping at my nose, I stood near the gate, sniffling and watching a parade of musicians accompanying the knights who were coming home from the wars. The traveling minstrels stopped just inside the castle wall, beneath a turret window. One played the kettledrum, beating out a mournful rhythm while a fiddle squeaked what sounded like a dirge. A feeling of foreboding passed over me.

"Livelier!" shouted a servant from the window as a mounted knight in full armor, the lord of the castle, clattered across the bridge. He sat stiffly, plate armor still strapped to his arms and legs. His velvet surcoat bore an embroidered crest, the yellow broom flower, and covered metal plates that had protected him from the deadly arrows of the longbows. Even though his helmet covered most of his face, I could see that he was bone weary.

Suddenly, as his white horse clopped past, the young Lord Robert fell heavily from his saddle and lay gasping on the threshold of the chapel. Hardly thinking, I pushed through the knot of villeins and serfs who had gathered around, smothering his air. I yanked off his helmet, and before anyone could stop me, I lifted his head in my arms, and marveling at the beauty of his fine features and the silver blond hair that draped my grimy sleeve, I pressed a pinch of foxglove under his lolling tongue.

Just as the bailiff grabbed me by the scruff of my neck, ready to throw me into the castle dungeon for touching a man so sanctified by station, Lord Robert sat up, took a deep breath, and looked at me.

"Praise be to God and Lazarus!" he said in a strong voice. "This young physiker has healed me! Bring her to m'lady!"

I was hauled off to the castle, washed, scrubbed, and fed in the courtyard. A woolen shift was pulled over my head, and soft leather shoes were placed on my calloused feet. My hair was brushed free of tangles and bound with a green ribbon. The dress given to me, who had always worn rags, was fit for a queen. Indeed, it may have been made for the lady, who in a sense was a queen, being the most highly placed female within a day's ride by horseback.

The gown was long and green and belted with a scarlet girdle. The sleeves were full and slit in six seams each, revealing from beneath a scarlet velvet inlay.

When I was brought before Lord Robert again, I kept my eyes cast down while Lord Robert addressed me. "There now," he said, sounding well pleased. "Thou art comely as well as possessed of rare healing gifts. Tell me what more you need for your healing arts and I will provide it. Young though you are, I give you the title of Wise Woman of Bedevere and you will heal the sick in my name."

Tongue-tied, I curtsied for the hundredth time and mumbled, "M'lord." I didn't tell him that if I were to invoke any name at all in healing, it would be the Savior's or one of his saints.

I was no witch nor ever would be. That much, Gallena had taught me well.

When I had stammered more thanks, he asked how I acquired my herbs. Terrified he would punish me for the truth or the lie, I chose the truth, "In his lordship's forest, my lord."

"But of course," he said. "Where else? Nevertheless, it will be more convenient for you to have an herb garden within the walls as well. I will order the cook to give you the kitchen garden and plant another for himself. Then you need not forage in the woods, where wild animals could attack you."

"My lord," I said, "please do not trouble yourself or the cook on my account. It is not difficult for me to find what I need in the wild. I am known for my knowledge of herbs," I added proudly. Then, fearing he might change his mind about the garden and growing bold, I added, "But I thank you for the garden, and if I could have a gathering apron, a large skirt with many pockets, I could manage exceedingly well."

"You will have your apron for the woods and the garden as well, where you may grow what you need and what pleases you." He then ordered a gathering apron made to my timidly given specifications.

I was stunned by his generosity and the tremendous change in my station. I could not say another word and just stood there, bobbing curtsies.

"Go with Dame Bewick now. She will take you to m'lady and then to your quarters." I glanced up and saw a woman so haughty and dressed so grandly that she might have been the lady of the castle. In that first exchange of glances we established a mutual dislike that was to last as long as we knew each other.

Later, I learned that though Bewick's manner was overbearing, her position was less impressive, and she was constantly trying to better her place by pushing herself forward. She fancied herself gifted in everything, including the use of herbs, and she disliked anyone she thought might be a threat to her advancement; she had no friends and was feared by all, even by Lady Isobel, Lord Robert's wife.

Dame Bewick brought me before the great lord's wife and her women, and they grilled me with questions: "If it be not magic, how does it work?" "Will it cure the dropsy?" "Did you learn from a witch?" "I cannot climb the steps for the pain!" On and on until I wondered if there was a healthy female within the walls.

With that first bath, I entered a world of

beauty and literally washed away my filthy old existence.

"Say now," said Lady Isobel when we were alone, "how came you to your knowledge?" Lord Robert's elegant wife might have been beautiful once, but her extreme thinness and sallow color told me that she had need of my healing arts.

"Very interesting," said Lady Isobel when I'd finished telling her my story. But there was something about the way she said it that told me she meant, I will wait and see how you do before I ask your help.

She flicked her hand at me, and I knew I was dismissed. I had yet to prove myself in her eyes. Later, I realized that she thought I might have magic power, but at the time I merely curtsied and congratulated myself on convincing her that I knew my trade and was not a witch.

Everyone was so impressed with my curing Lord Robert that I had truly become in a few short hours the Wise Woman of Bedevere. I was installed in the turret high above the place of my hovel, my former home. It all happened so quickly that it seemed like a dream, but when morning came, I was still in the castle, in my wedge-shaped room with one small window that looked out on the countryside I knew so well. Next to me, waiting to be placed on shelves that would be fashioned by the castle carpenter, were my herbs and Gallena's three drops of magic bouncing around in their clear container.

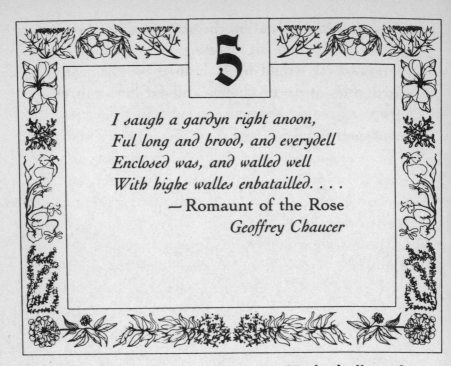

## 5

*I saugh a gardyn right anoon,*
*Ful long and brood, and everydell*
*Enclosed was, and walled well*
*With highe walles enbatailled. . . .*
— Romaunt of the Rose
*Geoffrey Chaucer*

THE COOK WAS A LAZY LOUT. He had allowed wisteria to cover the stone walls and weeds to crowd the beds of the kitchen garden that Lord Robert had given me. It took a month of hard work just to rid the place of unwanted growth. The cook hated me and gave me as little help as possible because Lord Robert had told him to plant his kitchen herbs elsewhere, in a small plot that had not even been tilled.

Lord Robert ordered his idle man-at-arms, Wulfstan, to help me with the heavy work, and although I cured a festering wound Wulfstan had received in a skirmish using a poultice of comfrey, he didn't like me either and worked grudgingly, considering it an unworthy task to do the bidding of a mere girl from even more humble beginnings than his own. He obeyed me only because he thought that I must be a witch, or how else could anyone so young work wonders? I did nothing to discourage his belief, because his fear was the only thing that gave me control over him.

My own garden stood directly back of the castle and had a stout wooden gate to which only I and the high lord himself possessed the key. The enclosure was rectangular, with raised beds forming part of the wall around the sides. Opposite the gate I ordered Wulfstan to build an arbor seat of oaken wood, and behind it I planted a richly scented Provins rose, which I trained to weave its way overhead and protect those that sat there from both prying eyes and diseases of the throat.

The potter made a large clay bowl that served as a miniature pond in the center of the garden. Around it, I grew hoary plantain, pheasant's eye, and sweet marjoram. The path around the center was made of pebbles from the Rushmore, the stream that flowed through the woods near the castle. The small paths that led from the center bowl, I planted with woodland thyme, which smelled sweetly when trodden upon.

In the raised beds I planted columbine, clove carnation, wild strawberry, lavender, thyme, rosemary, and many other herbs, some from seed and many already growing from the wild woods.

The whole design was a copy of Gallena's convent garden, which she had described so often that I had a clear picture of it in my mind. I drew the design on a piece of parchment supplied by Lord Robert, who approved each part of the project.

"You have great talent," he said to me. "Have you planted the herb that resurrected me from the dead?" he asked once.

"Yes, my lord, I will cultivate it carefully," I said. Foxglove leaf, for that was the herb, dried and powdered produced such a magical effect that when I used it I prayed God not to think I was trying to usurp his Holy Power or that I had found it among the Devil's plants. With this herb, I could raise the dead, and with continued treatment of wild carrot and dandelion powders, I could restore youth or, as in the case of Lord Robert, health, for he was still very young.

I could cure dropsy, spirit in-dwellings, heart stoppage, wind in the bones, and many other diseases, but even so, my skills were exaggerated, and I was venerated far beyond my merit. Dressed in my gathering apron, my herbs arranged in its pockets, I went about healing the sick and fearing my fall would be as spectacular as my rise or as the drop from my turret window to my former hovel below.

I thought often of Mother Barber and how easily people misread the signs, and I was very careful never to give the impression that I was anything more than a Wise Woman, under the protection of Lord Robert and Lady Isobel.

Although my garden's design had started as an exact copy of Gallena's convent garden, it soon became my own, changing and growing until I could no longer remember what Gallena had described and what I had invented. It seemed to me a magical place, a dream come true that not only provided me with the herbs I needed but a place where I could enter into the secret life of the herbs and watch them as they pushed their way out of the earth and grew in their mysterious cycle of seed to flower and back to seed again.

One day, not long after I'd started my garden and before Wulfstan had finished sealing the wall behind the arbor seat, I was watering the delicate shoots of lady's mantle, dropping the water slowly through my fingers so as not to disturb the frail beginnings of what was one of the most useful herbs to stop bleeding. Out of the corner of my eye, I caught a movement from behind the newly planted Provins rose. Without raising my head, I looked up and saw a small girl hiding behind the arbor seat, watching me.

There could be no mistaking her parent: she had her father's silver blond hair. I already knew that she existed, that her name was Elinor, that she was seven years old, and that Dame Bewick was in charge of her and hardly ever let her out of sight.

I made no move to show I noticed her, and she stood there until I heard Bewick calling. Then she slipped away, only to come back the next day at the same time, less guarded, as though she was hoping I'd notice her. But I was as shy of her as she of me, and I pretended to pay no attention to her. Each day she came closer, and each day I ignored her, until Wulfstan completed the wall that shut her out.

The very next morning I was summoned to Lord Robert, and there she stood next to him, her small hand placed possessively on his arm.

Elinor was slender and fair, with straight blond hair that fell about her shoulders like a sheet of silver rain. I thought she might have been the comeliest maiden I'd ever seen if she had only smiled, but her prettily shaped mouth drooped in a pout at the corners, and her large blue eyes were underlined with ugly dark crescents. I knew from looking at her that she did not eat or sleep properly.

I thought of what Gallena had told me, how the body is governed by four humors: blood, phlegm, choler, and melancholy. I recognized in Elinor the dominance of angry choler and cold melancholy.

I waited for Lord Robert to speak. When he didn't, I bobbed a curtsey and said, "M'lord." And then as cheerfully as I could, "Good day, young mistress!"

Elinor stared at me and her frown deepened. She raised her chin in an arrogant manner that reminded me of Dame Bewick and said, "Who are you?"

"My name is Ceridwen," I said proudly, as if she didn't know. "I am the Wise Woman of Bedevere."

"You're not old enough to be any kind of woman," she said so rudely that her father gave her a disapproving look.

"Elinor means," he said to me, "that you are not much older than she, and I have called you here because I think that, with your knowledge of the healing arts, you would make a most suitable companion for Elinor."

I did not like the idea of being in the company of a disagreeable child who thought she could order me around.

"Do you know what a companion is?" Elinor said in the same rude tone. I had not yet learned to control my temper, and she had exhausted my patience.

"A companion is someone to play with," I answered shortly. "A friend. But you will not have any if you are so disagreeable!"

Elinor's eyebrows shot up. Clearly, she was not used to being crossed. Lord Robert looked startled and then annoyed. It was not a good beginning. Before either of them could recover from shock, I tried to make amends.

"Never mind," I said quickly. "We will get on well. I know where there's a stork nest. Would you care to see it up close? There are two baby birds in it—just hatched!"

Elinor's eyes lit up, and her pretty mouth almost smiled. "Yes," she said sweetly, forgetting to be haughty.

"Then come with me. My room is at the top of the tower, and there's a window. You can scramble onto the roof and climb almost into the nest! The baby storks won't mind if you take care and don't frighten them."

I didn't need to say more. Elinor had left her father's side and was coming toward me. I grabbed her small hand, and we raced through the hall and down the steps, crossing the courtyard and coming breathlessly to a stop at the foot of the tower staircase. Elinor's cheeks were pink, and we both started laughing from the joy of running. I was beginning to like her better. I wondered if just having Bewick for a nurse was enough to spoil her humors.

"And now," I said dramatically, "I will say the secret password and the door to the tower will open magically so that we can climb the stairs to where the earth meets the heavens!"

"Really, Ceridwen?" Elinor asked, trembling with excitement. A small trick would do no harm at this point.

"Almost," I answered. "My room is so high that sometimes it pierces a cloud."

"What's the secret password?"

*Parsley, sage, rosemary, and thyme!*
*Open door upon hearing this rhyme!*

I'd made it up in a moment and was about to give the door a little kick, which Elinor wouldn't notice, when it swung open slowly with a creak.

Elinor's eyes widened, and I tried to hide my surprise.

The winding steep steps led upward through darkness. "Hold my hand and follow close behind me." Elinor put her hand trustingly in mine, and we climbed the curling narrow steps.

"Hug the wall side of the steps," I said. "They're wider." She was close behind me, clutching my skirt with her other hand.

"I can almost see," Elinor said bravely as we neared the landing at the top, which had a slit in the wall to let in light. "Do we need another password?" she asked as we stepped onto the landing and faced the door to my room.

"No. We are already in the secret place between earth and heaven, where all things are possible if only you believe." I was beginning to sound like Gallena, but I was enjoying myself as I watched Elinor. I felt sorry for her, really. Not only did she have Bewick for a nurse, but her mother was often sick and abed — in a way she was almost as motherless as I.

My room was wedge shaped, with one small window. I had set up, with Wulfstan's help of course, a table of smooth walnut wood made by Bedevere's carpenter to my specifications. I had a roller of the same wood that I used to grind the dried leaves until they were lighter than air. Six narrow shelves had been built for Gallena's twenty-seven bottles and seventeen vials, and a small recessed alcove for the Monarde. It was what I thought Gallena's convent table might have been like and as different from our old homemade, cross-legged table as I could imagine.

The table was on one side of the window, so that light shone on it. On the other side of the window was my bed, a wood frame filled with fresh reeds and covered with linen sheets, a gift from Lady Isobel. There was a built-in ladder that went almost straight up to another window in the roof.

"Hold tight and you can make it," I said to Elinor, pointing to the ladder. "I'll be right behind you. When you get to the top, there's a ledge on the outside where the nest is and where you can stand. Up you go!"

The stork was off foraging for food to feed her two babies when Elinor opened the window, and the baby birds opened their mouths expectantly.

"Oh, they think I am the mother bird," Elinor cried.

"Don't touch them," I said. "If their mother thinks we have touched them, she will carry them off to another place." It was something I'd always heard, but I had no idea if it was true.

"Ceridwen, Nurse Bewick says that storks are magical and that sometimes they are not birds at all but are really princesses who have been enchanted. What do you think?"

I didn't dare tell Elinor that I was sick of Bewick, who pretended to know everything. I had also heard a story about an enchantress who had turned twelve princesses into large birds.

"Some storks may be princesses," I said. I did not know Elinor well enough to tell her that I thought this stork was enchanted because it seemed to understand when I spoke to it.

We climbed back down to my room, and Elinor ran to the window, from which you could see the countryside all the way to the hills beyond the woods and, if you craned your neck, the sea on the other side of the castle.

"I would like to go there," Elinor said wistfully, pointing to the forest.

"I will take you with me some day when I go to the woods to find herbs."

"Could we go tomorrow?" she asked.

"We'll see," I answered, certain that Bewick would not approve. "Look, there in the corner. Those are the fresh herbs I have hung; when they have dried, I will roll them and store the powdered leaves in these little bottles. Sit down on my bed, and I will make you some chamomile and spearmint tea. It is good for you, and you will like the way it tastes."

There was a coal still glowing in my brazier, and after I'd brewed a small amount of tea, I sweetened it with honey and passed a cup to Elinor. She drank it as though she were sipping pure nectar.

"Thank you. It is very good," she said politely. "I am glad you are my companion." The pretty mouth made a sweet smile.

That first day with Elinor was so successful that I wondered if I'd ever have a moment alone again. She followed me everywhere until Bewick, furiously jealous, established all kinds of rules and duties to occupy Elinor with stupid tasks that did not interest her but kept her away from me. I suspected that Bewick's ambition was to be the Lady of Bedevere, and that Lady Isobel's ill health gave her hope. She did not want me in her way.

Only Elinor's mother and father held as firm a place in her heart as I. She loved her frail mother and adored Lord Robert. The circles under her eyes had disappeared, and she seemed a different child from the sulky, sickly one I had first met. I was proud that I had made the difference in her and that Lord Robert was satisfied with his choice of companion for Elinor.

"I am pleased with what you have done for Elinor," he said. "What treatment would you suggest for Lady Isobel to build up her health generally?"

"I would suggest she take a daily infusion of trefoil and chamomile, Lord Robert. And she should spend more time out-of-doors and less lying in her bedchamber surrounded by her ladies who speak only of their ailments."

As usual, I had been too outspoken, but Lord Robert looked startled for a minute and then said, "Please prepare the tea, and I will see to it myself that she drinks it."

Elinor came as often as she could to my garden, even when she was supposed to be doing something else that Bewick had devised, and my garden, surrounded by its high wall of honey-colored stone, flourished. I allowed no one in except Elinor and, of course, Lord Robert. He seemed to use the garden as a place to think and rest, away from the intrigue that surrounded him, the busybody women with nothing better to do than stir up rivalries and jealousies among themselves and invent gossip.

Sometimes Lord Robert came for a quiet talk,

and he always treated me as someone whose ideas were worth listening to.

"Ceridwen," he said one day, "what think you of Lord Warwick's use of our land for his own cattle grazing? Has he not enough of his own, that being the treble of ours? Should I lodge a formal complaint or will that stir up more trouble than it's worth?" Without waiting for an answer, which, indeed, I didn't have, he added, "It really harms me not that his white cows come through my woods to drink along the Rushmore, so perhaps 'tis best not to mention it lest it lead to further argument. I know you agree."

"Yes, my lord," I answered, for it did make sense to me not to create friction with a neighbor if no harm was being done by the cows.

Then he sat quietly, his eyes closed, his face to the sun. After a short while he stood, stretched, and walked purposefully away, forgetting to say good-bye to Elinor and me.

He often spoke to us about what he called "my gift for healing."

"It is not an ordinary gift," he said one day, looking at me thoughtfully. "Is there truly no magic in what you do?"

"No, my lord. I was only a motherless waif until Gallena, a Wise Woman herself, taught me the healing arts. I know nothing beyond that."

"You don't know who your mother was?"

"No," I said, afraid of how he might interpret my strange entrance into the world.

"She was found in a basket floating in the moat," Elinor piped up, pleased to be able to tell her father something he did not know. Foolishly, I had once told Elinor about the blue cross of Ceridwen and the boat-basket.

"Ah," said Lord Robert, "there is an ancient tale told about another Ceridwen. She was a sorcerer, and she put her child in a basket and set it adrift. Might there not be a connection?" Lord Robert watched me closely for my reply.

"I don't know any spells or enchantments such as a sorcerer might," I said quickly. "I am only a Wise Woman." I prayed Elinor would not tell him about the blue cross.

Lord Robert was silent for a moment. "And you have never tried to do magic?"

"*No!*" I said, frightened.

"There is good magic, Ceridwen," Lord Robert said quietly. "And maybe when you are older and understand more, you will study and find that your gifts go beyond those of a Wise Woman."

It was a frightening conversation, and I was happy when the subject changed.

Elinor loved to listen to anything I told her

about the herbs, and Lord Robert was pleased to have her learn. He told her that such knowledge would be helpful to her when she was a great lady in a castle.

"I am going to be a Wise Woman just like Cerri!" she said, and Lord Robert smiled and did not contradict her.

I took Elinor along the paths, naming each herb for her and letting her smell or taste the flowers so that she would become familiar with my plants and their uses.

"Notice this, Elinor," I told her. "It is angelica and you can tell it by its winged leaves and by its large umbels of yellow-green flowers that bloom in early summer. It protects against infection, especially against the Plague." I did not call that disease by its other names, the Black Death and Pest, because I did not want to frighten her. "But be careful, Elinor, not to confuse angelica with mandrake, which also has a yellow-green flower, because mandrake in excess can be a deadly poison."

I told her, above all, that if ever she were to uncover the root of mandrake and notice a resemblance in its shape to a small man, she must treat it with the utmost respect, covering it with earth once more and laying on top a dish of food suitable for a gnome.

I knew that I was sometimes talking over her head, but her solemn little face told me that she was absorbing everything I said. Someday she would need a knowledge of herbs to help her care for the people in her charge.

One day I told Lord Robert that I wished I could record my knowledge, and he asked me if I wanted to learn reading and writing along with Elinor.

"Oh yes, my lord!" I said. Only the monks in the abbey and fortunate members of noble families possessed such skill.

"Then I shall teach you both myself," he said. "We will meet daily at Prime in this garden, and our texts will be Lady Isobel's Book of Hours, which she wishes Elinor to have and . . . and this book that I had made for you as a token of my gratitude for saving my life and for being a companion to Elinor."

He handed Lady Isobel's book to Elinor, and to me he gave a similar book, the kind only the highest ladies of the land possessed. It had been made of the finest parchment by the monks in the Great Abbey. The Hours were written in an exquisite script, and the pages were deco- rated in gold, cobalt, and cadmium flowers, painted in borders around scenes depicting the months of the year. The feasts of our Lady and scenes from Christ's life were illuminated.

Many pages in both books were blank, so that we might fill them with our own paintings and words. My book was so beautiful that I was left speechless.

"Tomorrow at Lauds, then," Lord Robert said, and left.

Both Elinor and I learned rapidly to read and write. In one short season I could recognize the letters of the alphabet and puzzle out the words they made; in another, I was able to copy them into my book in words of my own. By the time winter came, I had written from my head all of the receipts Gallena had taught me as well as others I had learned from experience, and I had drawn and painted each herb next to the text that described its origin and use.

We were given a small amount of pigment and taught how to use it by Lady Isobel, who had painting skill. Elinor had inherited her talent, and her paintings were wonderful in color and detail for one so young.

My life seemed almost perfect: I was the Wise Woman of Bedevere and Elinor's companion. I tended the sick who lived within the castle walls; they had so many complaints that I seldom had time to venture beyond the moat. Except for the wealthy farmers, the peasants around the countryside and the village sick, whom I had once treated, now had to rely on their own knowledge or on old wives' tales, usually worthless. I was sorry for that, because I had made many friends before I came to live in the castle and I had liked helping them.

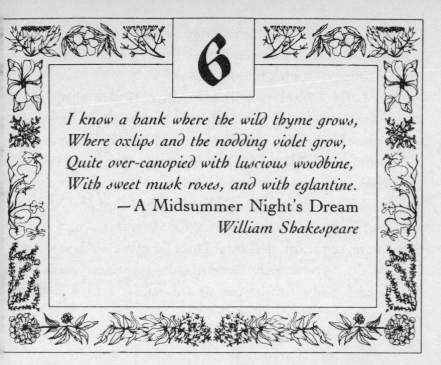

**6**

*I know a bank where the wild thyme grows,*
*Where oxlips and the nodding violet grow,*
*Quite over-canopied with luscious woodbine,*
*With sweet musk roses, and with eglantine.*
     — A Midsummer Night's Dream
           *William Shakespeare*

ONE DAY, LADY ISOBEL climbed the spiraling stairs to my room, surprising me with her visit and a problem that changed everything. She was out of breath from the steps, and her color was pale. When she had rested a moment, leaning heavily against the doorframe, she confided in me that ever since Elinor had been born, she had been unable to conceive the male heir Lord Robert wished for.

"The daily infusions of chamomile and trefoil have helped me generally, don't you agree?" I didn't, but I did not want to discourage her, and so I nodded. She continued, "But perhaps now we need to try something a little special, a little stronger. A charm, perhaps?"

Lady Isobel was not healthy, and I should have said, "I have no charms and no experience with this problem, and you must seek help somewhere else." Instead, I remembered that Gallena had told me that hartshorn mixed with cow's gall was believed to aid fertility but that she had not found it to be successful. I didn't want to seem ignorant in Lady Isobel's eyes, so I said, "I do have a very potent cure for barrenness. Come back tomorrow at this time, and I will have prepared it for you."

Three months later, when nothing had happened and Lady Isobel returned begging for a more powerful remedy, I should certainly have said, "There is no help for you, my lady." But Bewick came with her and listened in, a smirk on her mean face. I wanted to show off and prove how good I was, and so I said, "There are some stubborn cases, but I know of one thing that cannot fail."

"Oh, give it to me!" Lady Isobel cried. Bewick attended closely; she was not sure which side of the fence to hop on.

"What is it?" she asked suspiciously.

I knew of nothing, and so I said, "I need a day to prepare it. Come back tomorrow."

"Ha!" said Bewick, reading through my delaying tactics. "You have no such powerful charm. You merely wish to dazzle us with your tricks."

"I have no tricks! All of my herbs are blessed by God and I know their uses!" How was I to get out of this without ruining my reputation as a capable Wise Woman? Suddenly I remembered the mandrake root. Elinor had found one in the woods the day before, and forgetting what I had told her about being cautious and offering it a plate of food before disturbing it, she had yanked it out of the ground.

"Oh, look, Cerri!" she'd said. "It looks just like a little boy."

"Give it to me!" I had yelled. "We must make up to it for stealing it out of its place in the ground, or it will pay us back with a bad trick." I did not dare tell her that I had heard of one unfortunate woman who had died after accidentally dislodging a mandrake root. We had brought the thing back to my room and made a little dress for it out of Elinor's petticoat. Then we had given it an alcove on my shelf all to itself. I'd also heard that if you could get a mandrake root on your side, it was a powerful charm. I pushed aside Gallena's warning that came back to me: Do not believe old wives' tales.

"Lady Isobel," I said dramatically, "here is a charm that will bring about change." I presented her with the doll-like root, dressed sweetly in lace like a baby. "Treat it as a real baby boy for nine months. Place it in a crib and offer it daily the milk of a pure white goat."

I was making it up as I went along. I tried not to think of what Gallena might have said if she'd been listening to me.

Lady Isobel clasped the ugly root and cradled it in her arms, crooning to it as a mother might to her infant. She looked so filled with belief in my lie that I felt awful. If I could have taken it all back, I would have, but on Bewick's face was a look I read clearly: let Ceridwen commit herself to this absurd charm, and when it fails . . . why, the greater the commitment the harder the fall!

"I have never known it to fail," I bragged again. Never having tried it before, I was telling the truth.

"Let us hope, then," said Bewick delightedly, "that this time will not spoil your record."

The mandrake root worked — up to a point.

One month later, Lady Isobel burst into my turret room, where I was showing Elinor how to make a wreath of herbs that would protect her from sickness.

"I am with child!" Lady Isobel announced joyfully. Elinor was beside herself with excitement at the thought of a little brother, and I was weak with relief.

"When I grow up, I am going to be a Wise Woman," she went about saying to anyone who would listen. "How long does it take to learn the names of all the herbs?" she asked me.

"You've already started to learn, Elinor," I said. "It was you who found the mandrake root!"

"Will you teach my little brother about herbs, too, Cerri?" she asked.

"No, he will have to learn the manly arts," I answered. "He will learn fencing and jousting and things of that sort."

No one doubted that the baby would be a boy, and everyone in the castle rejoiced, except, of course, Dame Bewick, who remained silent with a smug expression pasted on her mean face.

Our happiness ended suddenly when Lady Isobel became ill. She lay abed, growing weak and strangely smaller rather than larger. I gave her teas that I hoped were beneficial and knew could not harm her. When none of them brought about a change, Bewick said, "Enough of your incompetence! I will cure Lady Isobel if you have not already cast a spell on her!"

"I didn't cast a spell!" I said, but I was afraid that what I had done with the mandrake root was worse than a spell.

The expected birth date arrived and passed, but still Lady Isobel did not deliver. All of Bewick's concoctions only seemed to make her worse. The midwife had come from the village and had moved into Lady Isobel's apartment. Bewick hovered over Lady Isobel like a giant vulture, constantly in attendance, claiming to know all kinds of wondrous cures from the nasty-smelling concoctions she brewed.

The midwife shook her head in dismay, and I heard her say, "I do not hold with this treatment. I have never had a case like this one, and I want no blame if the baby is not right."

Bewick said her knowledge came from her early training. She had been educated to be the wife of a great lord, but, as she never tired of explaining, the great lord to whom she'd been promised had been killed in a skirmish. She bragged constantly about what a great lady she might have been.

No one asked for more of my advice, but the

mandrake root continued to receive its milk and attention from Lady Isobel, weak as she was. "Let me hold the baby," she'd say, reaching out for the ugly thing. I could not bring myself to look at it. I was afraid of it.

Elinor was with me all day long, asking me questions, trying in her childish way to find a cure for her mother and the baby boy she still believed would come. I hoped desperately for a miracle and tried not to think of what might happen if the mandrake root failed.

One morning I took Elinor to the forest in search of something that we had not yet tried that might be good for Lady Isobel. We found a juniper tree deep in the woods and brought back a branch. I brewed a tea from its twigs for Elinor to offer to her mother.

"Here, Mother," Elinor said, carefully carrying a tankard across the room to her mother's bedside. "I found the juniper tree myself," she said proudly, "in the dark woods in a place where the rocks grow. It is good for you and the baby, and Cerri will burn the branch in the brazier. Cerri says that the smoke will prevent the fairies from stealing the baby and substituting a changeling."

"That idea went out of fashion with my grandmother," Bewick announced.

"It's not a question of fashion!" I said angrily. I had seen Elinor's face fall.

Lady Isobel smiled weakly. "Thank you, my dear," she said as Elinor held the cup to her mother's lips. "And thank you, too, Ceridwen. You have done so much for me." Lady Isobel stretched out her hand and drew me close. "If anything happens to me," she whispered, "take care of Elinor. You are still young, but she loves you like a sister."

Before I could answer, Bewick stepped over to the bed and heard me say, "I will never let anything happen to Elinor! But nothing bad will happen to you! The juniper smoke will —"

"It's too late for the juniper!" Dame Bewick said loudly. "Take Elinor and leave. M'lady's time has come!"

It was true. I saw Lady Isobel grimace with the first labor pain. The midwife hurried over, and I grabbed Elinor's hand and pulled her toward the door. "We'll wait in the garden, Elinor," I said, trying to keep the fear out of my voice.

Much later, I thought of that waiting time in the garden as the turning point in my life. I was beginning my fifteenth year, and until then I'd been content to be the Wise Child-Woman of Bedevere and Elinor's companion, the privileged favorite of Lord Robert and Lady Isobel. I was the envy of all. Why should I want more? Everything had been fine until Lady Isobel asked for a charm, and I gave her the horrible little mandrake root.

Elinor bounced up to me. She had plucked a lily of the valley. "Look, Cerri! Can we bring it to my mother?"

She had come into the circle of my arm and was resting her head on my shoulder. She was looking at me with such trust.

"Oh, Elinor! That is very sweet. But wait a bit, your mother is too busy with the midwife just now. Let's play a game of blindman's bluff!"

"No, that's a baby game! Teach me some more about the herbs. How do you know everything about all of the herbs? How long before I know as much as you?"

"I don't know quite everything," I answered, "but what I do know takes more than a year to learn—all day, every day, and most of the night." I was remembering how Gallena had waked me before dawn and kept me up memorizing half the night. "You can't do anything else but study all of the time if you want to be a Wise Woman."

"Can't you ever play?"

"Not really," I said, remembering how many

times I'd said to Gallena, "I'm tired. I don't want to do anymore," and she'd answered, "Then let's play a game. I'll name an herb, and you must draw it and tell me what its name means and how to use it. If you do well, then you may ask me a question, and I will answer with a story."

I had a piece of charcoal and had covered the hides that were my walls with drawings.

Gallena knew I loved her stories about when she was young in the southern mountains with her grandmother and later when she lived at the convent and worked in the garden. The stories always had something to do with herbs, and I realized now that in those days I was learning even when I thought I was playing.

And now? I had grown lazy. If occasionally I didn't cure someone with the knowledge I had, well, I couldn't be expected to succeed every single time. I was still treated with great respect because I'd brought Lord Robert back from the dead and cured others, though I was only a girl. Think what I might accomplish when I had a little more experience and was mature!

"Cerri, I told Nurse Bewick the story of how you cured Edith, and she said only a witch can cure a changeling. You aren't a witch, are you?"

"Elinor, you know that I am not a witch! If I were, I'd turn Bewick into a toad!" I was relieved when Elinor burst into laughter; I did not like to see her sad or having doubts about me.

The idea of Bewick being a toad was not only funny, it was tempting. What if I could transform things, like Ceridwen the Sorcerer had? Wasn't it worth studying? Elinor was still laughing. "Cerri, I wish you could do a trick like that. Do you know any tricks?"

"I don't do tricks, Elinor. Tricks are for witches. Everything I do has a good purpose." I sounded stuffy. "But I could do tricks if I wanted to," I added.

"Could you really turn Bewick into a toad? If you wanted to?"

"Probably," I bragged. What harm was there in trying a very small trick? Just to see if I could. And to amuse Elinor and keep her from worrying about her mother.

"Would you like to see me change that rose into a butterfly?"

"Yes!" Elinor clapped her hands.

Oh, I heard Gallena's warning this time, loud and clear and in her very own voice: "Never practice witchcraft! Never do any trick without a good purpose!" All of that went through my mind. "This is for Elinor," I said, ignoring my next thought, which was, For Elinor, eh? Not for Ceridwen to make her look good in Elinor's eyes? Tricks are no more than that — tricks — to fool someone into thinking the trickster is better than she is. They are illusions and have nothing to do with real transformations.

"Close your eyes, Elinor!" I said. When she did, I did, too. Then I spoke the words:

*Rose, rose, red against sky,*
*Turn into a butterfly!*

I reached deep into myself for the wish to make it so. Rose, I thought, spread your wings of petals and fly! My name is Ceridwen, and I have the power to change you! Rose, Rose! Become a butterfly!

Before I had time to open my eyes, I heard Elinor cry, "Look, Cerri! You did it! Cerri, you did it!"

There, fluttering close to where the rose had been, I saw a large butterfly. It was black and had rose red markings on its wings; at the tip of the wings was a lavender blue starlike shape just like the bloom on the rosemary bush. I had done it! It was a real transformation, not just an illusion! I tried not to let Elinor see how surprised and excited I was; I wanted her to think that I had known it would work all along.

Suddenly I saw Elinor's excitement die. She

was staring in back of me at the garden gate, which I had left open. Bewick was standing there, and I knew right away, just from the way she was looking at us, that something had gone wrong with Lady Isobel.

Elinor cried, "Oh, Nurse Bewick! Cerri made a butterfly! She really did! She said the magic words and turned the rose into a butterfly and . . ." Elinor's voice faded. "Has my baby brother come yet?" she asked fearfully.

Then, looking straight at me, Bewick thrust the mandrake doll at Elinor and said, "There is your baby brother — the only one you will ever have. Your mother died giving birth to — nothing!"

Elinor cried out as though a knife had passed through her and came sobbing to me.

"And you!" Bewick said to me. "You are a witch and this proves it!"

I felt Elinor tense in my arms. "Don't cry, Elinor," I said in her ear. "I promise you I am not a witch. Your mother knew that, and she gave you to me. I will take care of you."

"You will do nothing of the kind! Elinor does not belong to you. Lady Isobel was under your enchantment when she said such a thing! You may be able to make a butterfly, but you can't turn a root into a baby. You are a witch!"

I felt Elinor trying to wriggle away from me. "Elinor," I whispered. "Don't believe her!"

Bewick came close to me and put her hate-filled face in front of mine. "I will see to it that everyone knows what you have done, Witch-Child!"

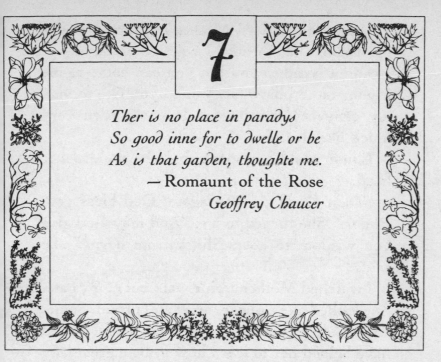

# 7

*Ther is no place in paradys*
*So good inne for to dwelle or be*
*As is that garden, thoughte me.*
— Romaunt of the Rose
*Geoffrey Chaucer*

I HAD ONLY MYSELF to blame for having lost everything I cared about. The day after Lady Isobel's entombment in the chapel, I kept to myself, afraid to meet the ones I'd wronged, but Lord Robert surprised me by bringing Elinor to my garden as usual. Lady Isobel's aunt Iraine, the mother superior of St. Agatha's, was with them. She had come to Bedevere when Lord Robert had sent word of Lady Isobel's death and was now preparing to return to the abbey. A short distance from the gate, Bewick was hovering like a vulture.

"Farewell, Elinor," Mother Iraine said, stroking Elinor's fair head. "I will not be far away. I cannot come to you but you can come to me if your father allows it. Would you like to visit my convent? We have a lovely garden very much like this one."

Elinor could not speak, but she nodded her head.

"Then I will see you again. God bless you, Elinor." She turned to me. "And may God give you wisdom to keep Elinor from harm," she said.

I watched Mother Iraine walk out of my gate. She looked like a queen, erect and proud. Someday, Elinor would look like that, and I would have helped her to learn how to be a great lady if Lord Robert let me continue as Elinor's companion.

Suddenly there was a loud banging on the gate. When I unlocked it, an exhausted messenger came in with Bewick close behind him. The messenger rushed up to Lord Robert, and falling to one knee, he said, "Forgive me, my lord, to intrude at such a time, but I come from the king. He has sent me to tell you that Baron Rogge is leading a force in an uprising. The king asks for your immediate assistance — as many men as you can muster to head the traitors off."

"Do not be concerned about Elinor!" Bewick cried. "Leave her in my hands! I will confine the witch to her tower until your return and I — "

"Enough!" Lord Robert said to Bewick. "Elinor, my dear, I must leave you, but I promise you it will not be long and I will return. You must be brave as every great lady must learn to be." He turned to Bewick and said coldly, "My lady was ill before Ceridwen came. Ceridwen is a talented Wise Woman and she will remain Elinor's companion." He looked at me sternly, and in that moment I would have died to prove his trust was not ill founded. He turned his stern gaze back to Bewick. "Dame Bewick, I leave the running of my household in your capable hands until I return."

Bewick swelled with pride, her first defeat forgotten. "But understand, madam," he added emphatically, "Ceridwen and Elinor will continue with their lessons. Is that clear?" Without waiting for an answer, he strode off with the messenger. "How many men in the uprising? Where are they now?" I heard him ask as the two men walked out of the gate.

"Come with me, Elinor," I said, brushing past Bewick. "Bring your book and you can paint a picture of rosemary in it. See, I have snipped this twig for you to copy."

Given a choice, she certainly wanted to be with me and not Bewick, but when she put her hand in mine, there was no happiness on her face. The dark circles under her eyes had returned, and she was in a world of her own, far from me. I knew that she grieved for her mother, but it was more than that. Her faith in me had been shaken.

We walked to my room without talking. I couldn't think of anything to say, and Elinor remained distant. Finally, I asked her if she still wanted to learn about herbs, and she nodded her head.

"If my mother had known as much as you do about herbs," she said, "she wouldn't have believed that the mandrake doll would make a baby brother for me. And if I had known, I wouldn't have let you give it to her!"

I blushed with shame. There was real anger in her voice. Elinor knew that I had made up the whole mandrake charm and that I had not cared enough about her mother to admit my ignorance.

"Elinor, you're right, and I am very sorry for

what I did. I didn't mean to hurt your mother, and I can never make up to you for her loss, but I can keep my promise to her, because she trusted me. I will always be your friend and take care of you."

"How can you do that if you're not here?" she asked, large tears forming in her eyes. "Bewick says that on St. John's Eve you will be the witch we burn on the hill."

A wave of fear washed over me, but I said as bravely as I could, "Your father knows that I am not a witch, and I will prove it by being a good companion to you. I will find my real powers, and they will be stronger than Bewick's evil ones, and I will not be burned as a witch!"

"Oh, Cerri! Can I help you look for your hidden powers? Do you think they are in the woods with the herbs?"

Elinor was looking at me with all of the trust she had once shown me, and I wanted to say, "Yes, we will find them together!" With just that short little lie, I could make up with her, but I had learned my lesson with the mandrake root.

"Elinor, Gallena said that I would have to study and work hard — alone." It hurt me to say that and see the look of disappointment on Elinor's face. "But I'll need you to be my friend

again. I can't study if I know you don't trust
me."

She put her hand on my shoulder and gave
me a small sweet smile. "I trust you, Cerri," she
said. It was the nicest thing that had happened
to me in a long time.

"Gallena told me that everyone has gifts, but
they don't know about them unless they search.
If you study and look for your own, we'll be
together in that way."

"I'd like that, Cerri, but I don't know what
I'm looking for."

"Yes you do! What do you want most?"

"I want to grow up and be a Wise Woman."

"Why?"

"So that I can have what I want."

"But what do you want?"

"I want to be the Great Lady of Bedevere
and take care of my father and my children and
all of the people of the castle and — "

"There!" I said. "You want to be Lady Elinor
of Bedevere, not Elinor, the Wise Woman of
Bedevere!"

"But I want to know about the herbs, too,
and I want to paint them in my book so that it
will be beautiful, but I don't know how to start,
Cerri." Her voice was getting weepy again.

"Why, the same way I do!" There I go, I

thought, making it up as I go along. But this time it was different from the mandrake root. This time the words came to me, and as I tried to explain it to Elinor, I was explaining it to myself, and I found I did know what I was talking about.

"Start with your painting," I said. "You are very good at that. Look at this sprig of rosemary with its little blue flowers. Count the different shades of blue in that tiny flower and try to capture them all in your painting. Then you will have made your own special magic."

While Elinor painted contentedly, I sat on the edge of my bed, holding the rosemary for her to copy.

Rosemary is for remembrance, the old wives say, and as I sat there with my eyes closed, I rolled the leaves between my fingers, smelling the pungent odor and remembering: I remembered Old Henne cutting an apple and handing me half. I could even smell the fresh clean slice, mingling with the rosemary. I went back further in memory and heard tiny wind-driven waves lapping at the sides of the boat-basket. I could see the snow-white hand that tucked me into the little boat and pushed it away from shore. A lady's hand. The boat landed with a tiny bump, and another hand reached down to me.

This time it was a rough peasant hand. Old Henne lifted me out of the basket and placed me in a wooden box, which smelled strongly of ale.

Was I imagining all of this? No, I am one of Ceridwen's daughters, with the power that comes down through the ages to us. I had always known that I was different, and now I knew what that difference was. I must learn the ways of enchantment, just as I learned the ways of herblore. I sighed at the thought of all the work and study that lay in front of me, but I wanted to keep my promise to Lady Isobel and watch over Elinor, and I would not be burned for a witch.

Dame Bewick was bound to obey Lord Robert's command and allow Elinor and me to study together, but she whispered to everyone that Lady Isobel's death was caused by "the mandrake spell cast by Ceridwen the Witch-Child."

The ladies of the castle were still friendly enough, because they needed me, but some asked me about the stories Bewick was spreading. I began to hear that she had accused me of raising storms and sinking ships, destroying crops, making cows go dry, and curdling cream. It was said that I had caused baby Agnes to throw fits by turning myself into an animal and flying around on a broomstick. If anything had gone wrong since I had come to the castle, Bewick said it was done by the witch-child, Ceridwen, up to mischief.

On St. Swithin's Eve, several weeks after our troop left, blue-black clouds rolled across the sky, and the day became as dark as night. God struck his earth with rods of fire and threw boulders across the floor of heaven. Once again there were rumors that the Black Death had found a ship and sailed across the channel to Britain. Fear was everywhere. I saw a procession of penitents praying that they might be spared a visit from Pest, and I stored a large supply of angelica, which would be in great demand if the Plague ever came to Bedevere.

That day, word was received that Lord Robert had defeated the enemy and was chasing them north; it was the first good news we had heard, and there was joy in the castle and the village. Our men would be returning soon, and we set about preparing a celebration. In a frenzy, Bewick ordered everyone around and, to my surprise, put me in charge of decorations and entertainment.

I was tying my gathering apron around my waist, hoping that the weather would soon improve and that I would be able to venture out, when I heard a slight cough behind me. There stood Dame Bewick at my door, having followed her unpleasant habit of appearing unheralded by footsteps. A bolt of lightning showed that her mouth, like a scratch across her face, was twitching, a signal that she was about to scold.

"Mistress," she said, addressing me and completely ignoring my name. "My little lady has lately been troubled by nightmares. Can you suggest a remedy?"

"Madam," I answered, "Let me take Elinor to the woods to gather the banquet greens. The fresh air will help her."

"She does not need to go gallivanting about the countryside with you. Please be kind enough to prepare a thyme infusion. I will return for it before midday."

"I can't do that, Madam," I said angrily. "As you have ordered, I am to spend this day preparing for the evening. When the storm has passed, I will go to the woods to gather the birch for the garlands and the St. John's wort for the destiny readings. Even if I were to search for the wild thyme and find it, I would not have time to prepare it. Let Elinor come with me; the rain-washed air is what she needs."

"She is too weary to tramp with you,"

snapped Bewick angrily. "Give me some St. John's wort, and I will make an infusion for Elinor."

I could hardly believe it! St. John's wort, as everyone knows, is much too powerful for a child. Not only can one read the future with its leaves, but a strong brew can cause the soul to leave the body. I guessed it was Bewick's intention to treat Elinor and then, if she behaved strangely, to tell everyone that I was at my spell-making again. Did she really care so little for Elinor, or was she that ignorant?

"Madam," I said as calmly as I could, "I beg you not to give Elinor anything. I will find some wild thyme and treat her."

"I will return for it then. Elinor comes tonight for the first part of the festival by order of her absent father, but she must leave before the reading."

"How can her 'absent' father order any-thing?" I asked with a sneer.

"The Lord Robert has sent a messenger ahead. He returns this very day and requests the presence of his daughter at the feast," said Bewick smugly, obviously pleased to be the bearer of important news of which I was ig-norant. "See to it that you have a soothing drink suitable for the child. I will ask it of you and test it myself." She turned to leave without waiting for a reply.

I wondered, not for the first time, what Bewick had been doing while she kept me occupied. Was it possible that she was meddling with my herbs? While Lord Robert was away, she had his key to my garden, and I remembered having the feeling that someone had rearranged the bottles on my shelves.

I did not keep my room locked, so that Elinor could come and go as she pleased. Had Dame Bewick been into my herbs while she sent me all over the place?

"Elinor rests," Bewick had been fond of saying, in order to block my entry to Elinor's room, or she had told me one of the ladies needed a medicine that required all day to prepare or a difficult search in the woods.

"The wife of Farmer Smith has a complaint." Bewick had said, picking a wealthy farmer's wife who lived outside the walls and far away. "Attend her this day."

Elinor's room was on the opposite side of the castle from mine. I had to cross the courtyard and go up one flight of twisting, dark steps to come to the hall that led into the various chambers occupied by Lord Robert's family and persons of high rank.

I knew Bewick was in the habit of going into the spinning room every morning, and so, after the rain abated and before going to the woods, I crossed the courtyard to Elinor's room.

The wind had died away and there was only a steady light rain. Elinor was lying rigid in her bed, with her eyes closed.

"Cerri, I know it's you," she said without opening her eyes. "I don't want to sleep. Nurse Bewick says I have to rest because my father is coming home tonight, but I am afraid I will have the dream."

"What dream, Elinor?"

"That the fairies have captured me, and I am surrounded by them. We are flying, and nothing looks familiar. I'm looking for my father, but I don't know where I am!" Panic mounted in her voice. "There are bad fairies everywhere, and when I want to fly on, they won't let me!"

"Oh, Elinor! Never mind a rest! Get up now and we'll find some wild thyme in the forest. I'll make a drink for you when we get back, and after you've seen your father, you'll sleep like a baby in the cradle of the new moon. But come with me now. It will do you good and me, too, to have your company."

That evening, the great hall was festive with the laurel garlands Elinor and I had picked and woven. Brocade dresses and metal ornaments reflected the light of hundreds of candles and torches. It was hard to believe that the small hours of the morning would see the splendor vanished and a motley crew of servants and villeins sprawled about the cold floor, sleeping as close to the dying fire as their rank allowed. For the hundredth time I thanked Gallena for her teaching and for setting me above the miserable lowly.

I sipped the sweet May wine from the wooden mazer handed to me by Lord Robert, who looked weary but was splendidly dressed. I sipped slowly, relishing the honor and the licorice taste that came from the fennel seeds I had added to the spicery larder earlier that week. I handed the bowl down the table to Wulfstan on my left and watched him gulp noisily before he shoved the mazer roughly to Bewick. Bewick accepted it fastidiously, careful to avoid touching his hairy hands.

She kept her thin lips together as she chewed and had such a worried look on her face that Elinor laughed from her perch between her father and me.

"Look at Dame Bewick," she whispered, giggling. "She is afraid to eat for fear of appearing vulgar. That is why she is such a stringy bean!"

And with that Elinor laughed so merrily that Bewick looked at us.

"Hush!" I whispered. I could see that Dame Bewick knew Elinor was laughing at her. She glanced accusingly at me, no doubt thinking I had made a joke at her expense.

I smiled at Bewick and nodded in a friendly fashion. She returned my nod stiffly and lifted her knife daintily to take a piece of venison from her trencher.

The minstrel was singing of a brave knight who slew a dragon but, on his way home to his castle and his lady, met a fair damsel in the woods and was bewitched by her. The minstrel was a talented storyteller with a beguiling voice, and he held his audience; I had never seen the great hall so rapt during a feast. There was only the sound of the player's harp, his captivating voice, and the occasional yelp of one of the hounds arguing with another dog over a scrap of food flung by a guest to the rush-strewn floor.

The candles cast long shadows on the high walls as the minstrel sang of the longing and grief of the lady, the wiles of the enchantress, and the lust of the knight.

Bewick stood up and said to Elinor, "Come, little lady. The hour grows late and the entertainment too bawdy for your delicate ears. 'Tis time for the readings and also time for you to be abed."

Bewick held out her hand, but Elinor jumped up and pressed herself against me.

"I want Cerri to put me to bed," she whined.

Dame Bewick grew red with mortification. "Come with me this minute!" she snarled between clenched teeth.

"Go, Elinor," I whispered, pushing her gently. "I'll come to you later."

But Bewick heard me. "That you will not!" she exclaimed in a fury. "You fill her head with nonsense! How can I control her when you tell her things no child should know and make her drink your witch's potions? I shall see to it that the true nature of your healing arts is exposed for what it is — witchcraft! Come now, Elinor!" She turned to Elinor, and something in her voice or my warning made Elinor obey. Meekly, she let go of my hand and walked demurely over to her father, kissed him, and with eyes cast down, left the hall with never a look for me.

I had no time to wonder what Lord Robert thought of the scene; suddenly the candles flickered and several went out, blown by the wind when the great doors opened for a troupe of mummers. The minstrel with the kettledrum beat a loud crashing sound and the dancers entered. Five led the parade. They were carrying torches and were costumed from head to toe in black garments that flew about them as they advanced rapidly to the staccato beat of drums. They wore masks painted with agonized white faces dotted with the dreaded red pustules of the Plague. The central mummer was dressed in tight-fitting black leggings and a jerkin; a white skeleton and a grinning skull was painted on his costume. There could be no doubt that he represented Pest, the Black Death, and the other writhing mummers were his victims.

The banquet guests sat without moving, frozen by the horror of the dance of Death. With grotesque movements, Pest wound among the guests, touching as many as he could while making his way to the head table. He moved so quickly that he reached Lord Robert before anyone had recovered from the shock of his entrance.

Lord Robert leapt to his feet and shouted angrily, "Seize the man! This is not fit entertainment for a time of merriment!"

No one moved. The dance was too convincing and had frightened the guests. When no one came forward, I rushed up, embarrassed for them all, and tore the mask from the leader. I turned to Lord Robert. "There, my Lord," I said. "No harm has been done. It is only play acting!"

"A thousand apologies, my lord!" cried the unmasked man, whom I recognized as Jack, one of the serfs who'd visited Old Henne's when I lived there. "A thousand apologies to you and your distinguished company, whom we only meant to entertain and honor for your victorious return . . . and to beg alms from your generous self."

I heard the sarcasm, although his words were accompanied by a great sweeping bow. But Lord Robert did not seem to notice the man's insult and relaxed slightly. "Leave quickly," Lord Robert said, "and use better judgement in the future. We do not need to be reminded of unpleasantness tonight." There was no mention of alms.

"Ceridwen," Lord Robert added in a voice I'd never heard directed to me, "if this performance was part of your entertainment, you may now escort the mummers out of the hall. Do not return."

"Oh no, Lord Robert," I cried dismayed. "I knew nothing of this! I . . ."

But Bewick had come back from putting Elinor to bed. "My lord," she said loudly for all to hear, "it was Ceridwen who planned this evening's entertainment! This is her doing. . . ."

Everyone started talking at once, and Lord Robert shouted, "Dear guests, return to your meal. The servers are bringing in the subtleties, and the mummers are leaving. Minstrel, give us a tune!"

Lord Robert turned his back on me as the music resumed with false levity. I stood in shock, but Wulfstan grabbed my arm and shoved me in the direction of the departing dancers. As we left the banquet hall, the guests gave us a wide aisle. The mummers had portrayed the Black Death convincingly and frightened everyone; there was not one person there who would ever trust me again. Thanks to my obedience to Lord Robert's command, and Bewick's unfortunate entrance at the wrong moment, I was blamed for this disgrace.

Outside, I turned on Jack. "You fool!" I cried. "Whatever possessed you to portray such an evil! You . . ." I stopped and gasped. He was standing wordlessly before me, but on his face I could see the beginnings of red pustules, the unmistakable mark of the Black Death. Standing before me, unmasked, was Pest.

"What cure have you for me, Wise Woman?"

he asked, grinning as wickedly as the skeleton mask he'd taken off.

"You are a dead man!" I cried. "I have no cure for the Plague when it has advanced so far. Why did you bring Pest to the banquet?"

"How can you ask that?" he said bitterly. "You were once one of us. You treated us when we were sick, but now you have no time. Our children go hungry while they . . . ," he gestured to the hall, "while those in the castle eat well and sleep in warm beds."

"What has that to do with it?" I asked angrily.

"If they will not share with us, then we will share with them!" He laughed, and then he began to cough and sneeze.

"Get out!" I cried. "Before Lord Robert knows you are what you pretend to be!"

I turned and ran back into the castle. I didn't stop until I reached my tower. I took the steps two at a time, and as soon as I reached my room, I tore off my dress and dusted myself from head to toe with angelica. I had touched the death mask. I had touched Pest!

I would have to leave Bedevere this night. If Pest did not get me, then Bewick would. By morning, they would know that Jack had died a Black Death and they would come for me, the witch who had brought the Plague to Bedevere.

Elinor was the only one who hadn't been exposed. It wouldn't be difficult for me to sneak
out alone, but I couldn't leave without Elinor.
There was nothing I could tell Lord Robert that
would make him understand that Elinor had to
go away with me.

I dressed quickly in my darkest dress and
cape and tied my gathering apron around my
waist. I stuffed my pockets with my herbs. I
tried to concentrate on a plan. I'd been studying
transformations, and although I was still far
from being able to slip in and out of forms, I
had changed the rose into a butterfly and could
manage illusions well. I could appear to be Elinor's great-aunt, the mother superior of St. Agatha's Abbey. With a little play acting and a
disguise, I could carry it off if I encountered
anyone in the castle.

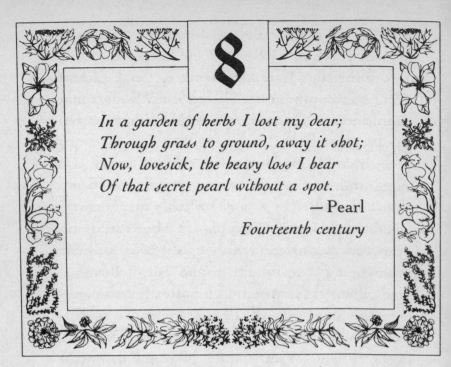

*In a garden of herbs I lost my dear;*
*Through grass to ground, away it shot;*
*Now, lovesick, the heavy loss I bear*
*Of that secret pearl without a spot.*

— Pearl
*Fourteenth century*

EVERY VILLAGE, EVERY PLACE where people lived together and moved about, would be visited by the Plague, but the convent was shut off from the world. Elinor would be safe there.

I tied a square of white linen around my head and another at my throat. With my cape wrapped about my shoulders and the hood pulled over my head, enough white showed to give me the appearance of a nun. I tucked my book into one of my apron pockets and checked to make sure that I had all of the herbs I used to carry whenever I went about the countryside treating the sick.

I allowed myself a moment to think of how dear to me my life as the castle's Wise Woman had become, and then I stepped over my garments that had brushed death, and looking around my turret room for what I feared was the last time, I closed the door and hurried down the stone steps. I watched for stragglers from the banquet, but the courtyard, lit by a full moon, was deserted; everyone was asleep in the main hall or in the apartments.

I tiptoed down the dark passage, staying close to the wall. Suddenly I saw someone walking toward me, carrying a candle. In its flickering light, I caught a glimpse of Dame Bewick's sharp features, but before I could duck into a doorway, I knew she had seen me. What was she doing away from Elinor so early in the morning?

I made the sign of the cross and turned in at the chapel door as though it had been my intention to observe Lauds at prayer there. I heard the chapel door open and close behind me and knew that Bewick had come in.

Throwing myself prostrate in front of the altar, I lay there face down and waited nearly half an hour praying I would hear the chapel door open and close again behind Bewick. There was silence. I rose to my knees, hoping to give the impression that I was going to continue to pray for a long time. The stone floor was cold and very hard and my knees hurt. Finally, I couldn't hold the kneeling position any longer.

I had to risk the chance that Bewick would see through my disguise, or I would lose the remaining minutes of darkness and be discovered by the entire castle.

Slowly, with a great show of piety, I rose to a standing position and, genuflecting deeply, turned. I took a deep breath and mumbled to myself:

*I am now the abbess; as I rise from my knees,*
*Let Bewick believe what she thinks she sees.*

There Bewick was at the back of the chapel, close to the door, obviously waiting to intercept me. I pulled the cape closer over my cheeks, and imitating the mother superior's dignified stride, I tried to sweep past Bewick. I felt an urgent tug at my skirt. I slipped into the pew and bowed my head in a listening, averted position.

"Iraine," she whispered urgently, "the saints

have sent you here, for I have prayed for guidance and was on my way to the turret to confront the witch, Ceridwen."

She paused, and I mumbled a noncommittal "Hmmm."

"It concerns the child, Elinor." She paused again but continued when I said nothing, "She chatters nonsense in an excited way all day, as small girls are wont to do, but of late she has begun to cry out in her sleep and babble hysterically. This very night she walked in her sleep — nay ran — to the window and throwing open the shutters cried to the moon, 'Cer-ee! Cer-ee, come to me!' I hastened to wake and calm her, but she would not be comforted and continued to call the witch. At last she quieted enough to drink a cup of lemon balm with a powder I'd prepared, and now she sleeps deeply."

Whispering to change my voice, I asked, "And is it so great a sin for the small one to call for the person she loves above all others?" Of course I should not have provoked Bewick's jealousy, but at least my words made such an impression that the timbre of my voice went unnoticed.

"You don't understand!" Bewick cried. "Ceridwen caused the death of your niece and has cast a spell on Elinor and on Robert as well! I think that at last he may suspect her, and I know enough about herbs to take care of all of us. We do not need a witch in our midst!"

Too upset to think, I answered, forgetting to disguise my voice, "And do you really fancy yourself to be a Wise Woman?"

Bewick started in surprise and stared at me. I pretended disdain and turned away, rising at the same time, and concentrating on dimming her vision and confusing her mind, I spoke haughtily, remembering this time to imitate the mother superior, "Beg God for forgiveness for your sinful jealousy and allow the Wise Woman to serve Elinor, and may God have mercy on your wicked soul."

I left Bewick with her mouth open in astonishment, too stunned, I hoped, to question my identity. Did I have time to get to Elinor before Bewick returned to her duties, and could I slip out of the castle before everyone woke at dawn? I did not allow myself to think what Lord Robert would do when he found out that Elinor was gone. I hurried to Elinor's room, careless of who might see me.

I found her bed empty; she was standing at the window staring through the torn parchment at the stars. Her face was a mask of fear, but softened when I spoke her name.

"Cerri!" she said. "Why are you dressed like that? You look just like Tante Iraine!"

"I am playing a game," I said, counting on how much Elinor loved games. "Would you like to play, too? We will pretend that I am your great-aunt and you are a tiny foundling left in the pass-through at the convent gate." I made it up as I went along. "We will go to the convent and see if we can fool the good sisters. Would you like that?"

"Oh yes!" cried Elinor. "We will fool them and get inside the secret garden and maybe the convent itself!"

"Then first we must make you look less like a princess and more like a waif." I ripped off the lace hem, leaving Elinor's nightgown ragged at the bottom.

"Here," she said, entering wholeheartedly into the spirit of the game as she always did. She rubbed the soot from the candle on her gown and her face and turned expectantly toward me.

"Good! Now we must do something to hide your hair."

Without hesitation, Elinor ran to the brazier

and dipped her small white hand into the ashes. Handful after handful she rubbed into her hair until it was dull and dirty.

"Now," she said, a pleased look on her face, "am I not disguised?"

"Yes!" I said. I saw in her something of myself as I must have looked when Old Henne kept me, Waif.

"Quick," I said, "before anyone wakes!"

We hurried out the door and slipped through the castle and across the yard to the gate, just as Old Henne, bleary eyed, let down the bridge for the cattle to cross over into the fields. Once out of the castle, I no longer practiced the illusion of being Mother Iraine, and I saw Old Henne look at me twice, recognition close to the surface of her fuzzy mind.

Walking rapidly, we crossed the bridge as the sun showed its round eye over the edge of the earth. Lord Robert's castle, Bedevere, standing high, made a dark silhouette against a pink sky. I wondered if I'd ever see it again. I felt a lump in my throat; once again I was a homeless waif.

After we'd crossed the bridge, we descended into the valley and the lush meadow where the cattle were already grazing near a few farmhouses clustered together. Past the meadow was the forest, with the Rushmore running through it, and on the other side of the forest the hills began.

We didn't slow down until we'd reached the banks of the stream. Then we dropped in weariness. I didn't dare linger; I knew there'd be a search party out as soon as it was discovered that Elinor was missing. The clues I'd planted to make them think she'd only gone with me to gather herbs wouldn't deceive anyone past midday.

It was then that I made a terrible discovery: I had lost my book, and unbelievably, I'd forgotten the Monarde!

The book could be in only one place — the floor of the chapel, having slipped out of my pocket when I lay prostrate. But the Monarde, with its three drops of magic, was where it always was, in a corner on my shelf, now lost to me forever. Feeling as though I had lost my identity, I knew that we had to go on.

"Cerri, what is wrong?" asked Elinor, tugging at my skirt.

"Nothing," I answered as cheerfully as I could.

"I'm tired of this game, Cerri," whined Elinor. "Let's bathe in the stream!"

Elinor kicked off her shoes, pulled off her dress, and waded in before I had time to say no. She was used to having her own way. She looked so happy and carefree, splashing water and laughing at the drops, that I couldn't resist joining her. I kept my dress on but took off the nun disguise and waded to a spot near her.

Just as I was about to tell her that we had to hurry, Elinor slipped on a rock and fell, bruising her rib and making a nasty cut. She cried as much from fright at the sight of blood as from pain. Quickly I applied a poultice of comfrey and held the compress tight against the wound. We were losing precious time, but I had to stop the bleeding. There would be a little scar, but I knew it would heal.

"Look, Elinor," I said to cheer her up. "You will have a mark on your rib just like mine. Does it hurt anymore?"

"No. You are a good Wise Woman!" she said. "Let's go to the convent!"

Past the last line of trees, we came to the hills; St. Agatha's convent was not an easy journey by foot for a small child. The hills were as barren as the valley was verdant, and we trudged along another mile over the rocky surface until we came to the convent. The convent's high walls made it a fortress as impregnable as a castle, although without soldiers to patrol its ramparts. Instead, it relied upon the power of the Almighty. If people feared the power of witches, they feared even more the power of those who represented God on earth.

The sun was casting a rosy glow on the sand-colored stone of the convent as Elinor and I crossed the top of the last hill and stood looking across at the forbidding wall.

I tried to imagine the scene at Bedevere. By now they would know that Elinor and I were gone and that Pest was among them. I wondered if Lord Robert would guess why I had taken Elinor and where. I doubted it. If he believed that I was a witch, he probably thought I had stolen Elinor for the fairies and would never guess that I'd come to the convent.

We heard the sound of a bell and knew that we had been sighted from the priory and that the nuns were alerted that visitors from the out-side world were approaching their gates.

Lord Robert had carved a whistle from a birch branch that Elinor wore around her neck, and I told her to sound it now. She blew, and its tone told the abbess that one of the visitors was her grandniece. Elinor ran down the hill, hair flying. I walked sedately, watching the heavy wooden gate swing slowly open.

Arms outstretched in greeting, the abbess enfolded the flying child against her bosom. She looked over Elinor's head at me and nodded her permission to enter.

"Elinor, my dear, go with the prioress to the kitchen. We have just baked seed cake."

Elinor skipped off and the abbess turned to me. "Ceridwen?" she asked, putting into my name the question "What is of such great importance that you break into our life of prayer?"

I curtsied and said, "Mother, the Black Death is at Bedevere."

"Come with me, my child," she said without hesitation. "We will talk in my office where none can hear us."

We hurried along the covered walkway and dark halls of the convent into the abbess's spacious office.

"And why is it that you bring only Elinor?" she asked as soon as the door was closed.

"Mother," I answered, "everyone except Elinor was exposed. It was the only way to protect Elinor. Lord Robert sent me," I lied.

She nodded her acceptance of my explanation. "How can we keep the Plague from St. Agatha's?" she asked.

"The rules of your contemplative order that forbid contact with the outside world are your best prevention; they can save you if you are strict and let no one enter these walls," I answered.

"Will you return then?"

"No," I said, thinking quickly. "I can help you here if you will let me. It is too late at Bedevere."

"Tell me, then, what shall we do?"

"You mustn't let anyone in at the gate, and you must not even buy food from the villagers or milk from their cattle. You must live as though you were the last people on earth, depending on nothing outside your walls, because once the Plague finds one of you, no one is safe."

"And can you help us with your herbs?" she asked, her quick mind one step ahead of our words.

"I know of herbs that discourage the Black Death, and I brought with me some of my own. In your garden I will find others that can be used if you let me work there."

"There is a cell left vacant through the recent death of one of our most ancient nuns. It has been made ready for a postulant due to arrive next week. She will be notified of a delay, and you shall have her place. It will cause less of a stir if you wear the postulant's veil." She rose. "You may tend the garden. Act your part," she said. "Who knows, you may find you have a vocation." She smiled at the improbability of her words, but they were not without sincerity. "Go with the prioress to the novitiate for your habit. I will see to it that no one comes into your cell, and you must ask me for what you need to prepare your medicines. Your duties will be those of gardener for our medicinal garden."

She paused, looked down, and said surprisingly, "Ceridwen, I have my own reason for trusting you. I do not like the influence of Dame Bewick. Is there something more you need or wish to say?"

"No, Reverend Mother," I answered, "except that I am most humbly grateful for your trust and care."

"Never mind that," she said. The moment of intimacy vanished. "It is for the good of the community and for Elinor that I act." She pulled the bell cord for the prioress.

And so it was that Elinor and I came to live within the walls of a convent. Elinor slept alone in a small room near the prioress, and during the day, the prioress kept her busy. I saw little of her. I was successful both in my masquerade as a postulant and in keeping the Black Death away. We were completely sealed off from the world; none of us left the cloister. Nor did anyone from outside pass through the gate.

Posing as a postulant, I was careful to observe the rules of the convent, especially the rule of strict silence. It was just as well: the nuns were ladies, all twenty-four of them, from great houses, and my humble beginnings would have betrayed me in speech. A convent was not for the likes of Waif.

I had to laugh, silently of course, at how the ladies, deprived of speech, invented ways to communicate. There was a babble of facial expression and waving of hands at mealtime, made hilarious by someone desiring milk and going through the motions of milking a cow or "Please pass the fish!" translated by a wagging of hands mimicking the tail of a fish. The silence was broken only by the lector, reading a pious work at midday while we sat together in the refectory eating. Elinor ate separately, fed by the cellaress.

Occasionally, Elinor slipped away to join me in the garden, where I worked daily throughout the afternoon, until vespers and supper. There she chattered away in a whisper, and I replied with nods, smiles, or frowns. She was happy, spoiled by the prioress and the cellaress, who vied for her affection. When she asked for her father, I lied once more and said that he had gone again from Bedevere in service to the king and would send for us when he returned.

I did not mind the orderly, contemplative life of prayer and thought. I liked the carefully laid out manner of existence, the day and night punctuated by Prime, Terce, Sext, None, Vespers, and Compline, and I liked the cellaress, who supervised my work in the garden and took care of the food and the servants of the abbey, one of whom helped me dig, plant, weed, and harvest. Best of all, I was improving my skills in sorcery. I could concentrate deeply and create an illusion. One day I made a flock of yellow finches, nesting in the fruit-laden quince tree. The cellaress caught me at it, but I changed the birds back into quinces so quickly that she must have wondered whether she had hallucinated.

My bare cell, with its narrow cot, suited me well, and it did not disturb me to rise at two in the morning for Matins in the choir. But one moonless night, I heard the thin wail of an infant. I dressed quickly and ran to the entrance. There was a baby in a basket lying in the pass-through, the small opening in the wall used for deliveries so that the nuns, vowed to contemplative silence, could receive goods from the outside without distraction.

As the prioress, with Elinor close by, lifted the infant, its blanket fell away, and under its thin arm I saw the unmistakable round pustule imprinted by the Black Death.

"Don't touch it!" I screamed, but Elinor had already taken the baby in her arms.

"My baby brother!" she said.

The nun spun around startled at the sound of a voice within the cloistered walls. I had broken the primary rule of the convent. I had not only spoken, I had yelled!

In a matter of seconds we were surrounded by nuns with lighted candles. Mother Iraine walked into their center, took the infant from Elinor, and pushed her toward me.

"Go to your rooms," Mother Iraine said, and the nuns turned as one and hurried silently back to their cells. She turned to me. "Take Elinor and leave immediately. If she survives, you must bring her back to Bedevere. That is where she belongs. I have learned that Lord Robert was spared and is looking for his daughter."

I could tell by the way she spoke that Mother Iraine knew about my lie. "You must stay with her and help her to deal with Dame Bewick. Do you understand?"

"Yes, Mother," I answered. "But please! Do not hold the Black Death in your arms! Place the infant back in the pass-through, and I will give you masterwort and angelica. You must burn your clothes and those of the sister who first — "

"Didn't you hear me!" Iraine said. "You know as well as I that it is too late for me. We will not meet again in this world." She blessed me and then Elinor. "Go, dear Elinor, and may God go with both of you."

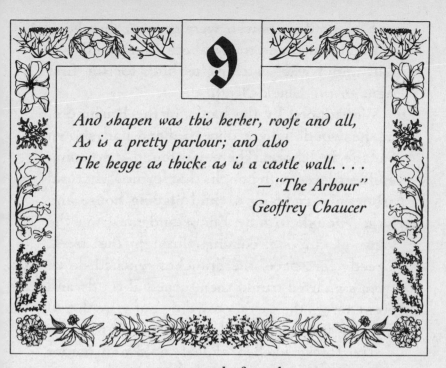

*And shapen was this herber, roofe and all,*
*As is a pretty parlour; and also*
*The hegge as thicke as is a castle wall. . . .*
— *"The Arbour"*
*Geoffrey Chaucer*

WE LEFT THE CONVENT before the sun came up, and by noon we had burrowed deep into the woods. Now there was no safe place from the Black Death or from Lord Robert, whose soldiers must be tramping over the land at this moment looking for Elinor and the wicked witch who'd stolen her.

I knew that even if Pest had finished his dirty work and left Bedevere, Bewick was still there. Mother Iraine had heard it or she would not have warned me to protect Elinor from her. I feared Bewick as much as the Plague. I could not go back until my powers were stronger than hers.

I had dosed and dusted both Elinor and myself, and I was watching us both for the first signs of the Black Death.

We stopped by the banks of the Rushmore, in the woods where once Gallena had shown me the hellebore. There we found a weeping mulberry tree with boughs that formed a natural arbor, just right for a child playing house and large enough to hide Elinor and me from the view of anyone coming through the trees. Greedy for space, the branches reached down from a gnarled trunk, then turned abruptly and crept across the earth, crowding out growth and forming leafy walls and a soft floor of moss.

The forest smelled of leaf mold and tender shoots bathed by the Rushmore's clear water, and the Plague seemed very far away. Barefoot, Elinor wiggled her toes, curling them around the smooth pebbles that lined the banks, pushing at the round rocks lying like thrush eggs in the creek's bed.

"Cerri, I want to go home," she whined. I had explained to Elinor that the baby was an abandoned child carrying the Plague, but seeing that poor doomed baby had made Elinor think of her mother, and she was homesick.

"We're going home," I said. "But first, we have to hide from Pest in the woods until he tires of looking for us."

"But my father will keep him away if we go home to Bedevere. I miss my father! Cerri, I hear boots breaking the little twigs! Now they are sloshing through the stream!"

"Quick, Elinor! It may be villagers with Pest! Run to that tree!" I said, although I knew it had to be Lord Robert's men. We climbed a gigantic oak, hollowed where its great branches parted, and lay snug while the pursuers tore the underbrush and shouted to each other.

I held my breath as they searched the place where we'd been, but they did not pick up our trail and continued on. I did not like lying to Elinor, but I had to make a plan before I brought her back to Bedevere and Bewick.

The hollow in the tree led into the trunk's interior, a tiny, dimly lit space as cozy as a chamber. I made a small bed of dried leaves for Elinor, and when she had fallen asleep, I went quietly through the forest, gathering berries and dandelion leaves and blessing Gallena, who had taught me how to live from nature.

Dawn came slowly into the trees. The day that followed was gloomy with mist.

"When are we going back, Cerri?" Elinor asked as soon as she awoke. "I'm hungry."

"We will have our meal first," I said, playing for time. I cooked a hare I'd trapped during the night, and careful to obliterate all traces of my small fire, I fed Elinor some of the sweet red meat with wild strawberries. While we ate, I thought: The ancient warrior Celts, who once lived in this forest, had dyed themselves blue to make themselves invisible to the invading Saxons.

"I know a game!" I said. "We will make ourselves invisible! Would you like that? You will see everyone, but no one will be able to see you!"

"Oh yes! Make me invisible!" Elinor said, delighted.

"Look, I have brought woad paste with me — enough ointment to turn both of us into blue shadows!"

I rubbed the paste on Elinor's fair skin and watched her blend in with the shadowed forest. I told her how terrifying it must have seemed to the invaders to see part of the forest disengage itself from the trees and rush at them brandishing clubs and spears and shouting their fierce battle cries! And when the Celts wanted to remain hidden, what better disguise than to become shadows?

But this was just a delaying tactic. I had to bring Elinor home if she did not come down with the Plague. Lord Robert would protect Elinor from Bewick, but would he protect me from her and from all of the others who thought I was a witch? I shuddered. What could I do?

Elinor laughed as I rubbed woad on my face. "Oh, Cerri!" she cried. "Will I fly? You look just like the Virgin ascending into heaven!"

"Don't blaspheme, Elinor! What are you talking about?"

"In my mother's hour book there's a picture of Mary dressed in blue standing on a cloud. She's going up to heaven, and she's blue all over, even her face! Dame Bewick says witches' ointment is blue, too. The blue is what makes Mary fly up."

"What nonsense!" I said. "That painting is just the way the artist portrayed our Lady. And Dame Bewick doesn't know anything about witch ointment."

"Yes she does!" Elinor said imperiously. "Dame Bewick says that flying ointment is blue and that it's what makes witches fly, and she's tried it. It's true."

"Bewick has flown!" That proved it. She was dabbling in the witches' garden, and she was tampering with my herbs. "Mary was not a witch, Elinor," I said. "She was the mother of our Lord. She didn't need magic to ascend into heaven. I am painting us blue so that we may move about in the woods invisibly."

"Cerri," Elinor was serious, "Dame Bewick told me once that she could prove you are a witch if she could throw you in the water. She says she's seen you swim and only witches swim. Can you swim?"

"More nonsense! Of course I can swim. I learned it almost as soon as I learned to walk, and so did the other brats who lived by the moat and wanted to cross it. Listen carefully, Elinor," I said, "I have been teaching you everything I know, everything I was taught by Gallena and all that I have learned since. But none of it is magic nor is it evil. The power in the herbs is blessed by God. But witchcraft is evil and comes from the Devil.

"Gallena gave me one bit of fairy magic, and it is still in a dark corner of my shelf. She warned me to use it only in a desperate situation if all else has failed, because it can only be used once. Then she told me a riddle. She said it gives both life and death."

"Did she mean it would kill you?" Elinor asked.

"I don't know. All magic has a heavy price, and since I have never been desperate, and since it can only be used once, I have never wished to use it and do not know the answer to the riddle. It is called Monarde . . ." I had been about to add, "and I can never go back to get it," but I did not want Elinor to know that.

"Cerri, what is a desperate situation?"

"If you were about to die, that would be a desperate situation," I answered promptly.

"I'm too young to die," she said carelessly, pulling up her shirt and revealing her bony midsection. "Are you going to paint my stomach blue?"

"What is that?" I cried. Right over the tiny scar from her fall, I saw a small red bump. Oh, God, I prayed, let it be an insect bite and not the beginnings of a pustule!

"It's my scar! You know that!"

"Of course," I said, too frightened to be clever.

Elinor began making a game out of pretending to be a flying witch. She was very convincing, but I put an end to it. I was suddenly sick with a terrible foreboding of death.

That night I looked at her stomach again but

the red bump was no worse. I dosed her well with angelica and tried to sleep.

The next morning, while Elinor and I were still deep in the tree, I heard a sound, and peering out, I saw Lord Robert, who, eyes to the ground, was following my tracks.

He was dressed in hunting clothes and looked a part of the woods itself. His tall slim body was covered in a belted tunic made of soft fawn leather, and his legs were encased in green hose. He had on deerskin boots, and slung across his back was the bow and quiver of arrows he had made in my herb garden while Elinor prattled away to keep us company.

His silver blond hair caught the rays of sunlight that penetrated the thick leaves overhead; his sharp gaze missed nothing, and he walked as silently as a shadow. I saw him stop, stoop down, and pick something up. Too late I realized it was Elinor's shoelace.

"Ceridwen!" he called. "I know you're there! What have you done with her?"

Elinor looked at me imploringly, but I shook my head violently and put my finger to my lips. He was staring at our oak tree.

"I won't hurt you, Ceridwen; I'll not even punish you, but you must tell me where she is."

I put my hand over Elinor's mouth. "Hush!"

I whispered, but she was too quick for me. In one movement she slipped out of my grasp and called in her high-pitched voice, "Here I am, Father!"

In seconds he climbed our tree and stood in the fork looking down at our lair. His startled, angry look at our blue faces told me what he thought.

"What enchantment have you put on Elinor?" he asked.

"None!" I said. "I'm not a witch! I would never harm Elinor!"

"Whatever your reasons," he said, "I should have heard them before you took my child. Come, Elinor."

I will never forget that she hesitated before obeying him. She looked at me, and I knew she wanted my approval. I shook my head again, and she turned sadly to her father and climbed up to him.

"No!" I cried, standing up.

Why didn't I argue? Something as strong as a spell prevented me from explaining and deprived me of speech — even of a logical thought.

"Don't try to come back," said Lord Robert, holding Elinor tightly. "I will have you burned for the witch you are. Many died at Bedevere because of your wickedness. Letting you go free now is my last payment to you for having saved my life so long ago."

Elinor gave a little cry and reached out to me. Her shoe with the missing lace fell off and into my extended arms as Lord Robert jumped with her to the ground and ran. I listened as his footsteps faded, and then there was a single sound, muffled and distorted by distance. It sounded like a loud sneeze, the second symptom of the Plague, following the pustules. I fell back into the hollow of the tree and sobbed myself to sleep. Pest had caught Elinor and would have me, too, by morning.

**10**

*Ring-a-ring of roses*
*A pocketful of posies*
*Atishoo! Atishoo!*
*We all fall down.*
*—Medieval folk rhyme*

A STRANGE LISTLESSNESS came over me as I waited for Pest to find me. Elinor had been caught and I was next. I couldn't make up my mind which was worse, dying the Black Death or being burned for a witch.

I seldom left the tree hollow, living on berries gathered less than half a league away and drinking the cool water from the nearby Rushmore. I dreamed both asleep and awake; my waking thoughts wandered aimlessly, as illogical as my dreams.

I dreamed that I could fly without wings; I

used a swimming breaststroke through the air and soared safely over the moat toward the castle and away from someone who was chasing me. I ran through a series of rooms in the castle, looking for my real mother to protect me, but before I could find her, a wicked enchantress cast a spell over me. I smelled smoke. A witch was about to be burned at the stake. The witch was me. With all my will I tried to escape, and awoke sitting, drenched in sweat and filled with terror. I didn't want to sleep again and slip back into that dreamworld.

Half-awake, I remembered a game called hoodman blind, which I often played with Elinor, and another — ring-a-ring — the game she loved best. In her child's voice she'd sing a rhyme:

*Ring-a-ring of roses*
*A pocketful of posies*
*Atishoo! Atishoo!*
*We all fall down.*

I could see her, dancing in a circle, completely given over to the joy of the game, her small body leaping her hair flying around her happy face, her enthusiastic tumble to the ground.

But I didn't like to see her play ring-a-ring because the childlike rhyme is really a description of the phases of the Black Death. The ring of roses are the red circular pustules that cover the bodies of Plague victims; the posies are the nosegays carried by people in the hope that the odor of flowers will ward off the disease. "Atishoo" is a sneeze, one of the first symptoms of the Plague, and "We all fall down" means death.

Gallena had taught me that sweet-smelling posies do nothing against the Plague; flowers do not even overpower the stench that rises from the dying. The worst part of the sickness must be knowing that each stage will be followed by something more horrible until the body turns black and dies.

It takes only four days from the first sneeze until death comes. Had Elinor already tumbled down, overcome by the Black Death? I could find out if I went back to Bedevere, but the fear of burning and knowing that no one there believed in me held me tighter than a rope or a spell.

Three days after Lord Robert took Elinor away, I began to feel ill and knew that if I pulled up my shirt, I'd see the telltale sign. Suddenly, I wanted to live, or at least I didn't want to die a Black Death.

I began to think of what I might do, and I

remembered having seen mistletoe growing at the top of the oak tree that had become my home. Gallena had told me that mistletoe was also called all-healer. "Use the leaves," she'd said. "The blossom brews sticky. If gathered on the sixth day of the moon of St. John's Eve, it will cure anything." I knew it was well before St. John's Eve, but I had learned that the right herb often worked no matter the day it was gathered.

I had forgotten how good it felt just to do something. Up, up I climbed, until I was near the top of the tree and on a level with a bough of mistletoe that clung to the very end of a small branch.

I reached far out. The branches swayed as I touched the bloom. My fingers closed on a tiny twig, and I pulled it close enough to dislodge the glossy leaves with their pearllike berries, the all-healer, mistletoe.

When I looked at the ground it seemed very far away. I don't remember climbing down or brewing the mistletoe. My next memory is of waking up curled in the hollow of the oak, with no idea how much time had passed. I knew I'd survived what must have been an attack of the Plague, and an empty gourd that smelled of all-healer was proof that the mistletoe had not been a dream.

It would have been easier just to lie there and drift away into nothing, but now, my mind was made up. My victory over Pest gave me confidence. I longed to go back to Bedevere and find out what had happened to Elinor.

I forced myself to search for food and to eat, bathe, and gather my strength. Then one day, close to the summer solstice, when the days are long, I awoke and felt the sun, shining through the leaves, warm on my face. The joy of health had returned. I spent the day gathering fresh herbs and bathing in the Rushmore, and the next morning, before light, I set out for Bedevere. I crossed the moat at the first lowering of the bridge and made my way carefully across the castle grounds.

I walked around the back of the chapel, past the kitchens and toward my garden. A whole season had gone by since I had last seen it. The sturdy wooden gate, which I had always kept locked, was ajar and hanging by one hinge. I shoved it open and went in. All I could see were weeds. My precious herbs, always full and green and so carefully nurtured, had become choked with ugly growth; some herbs had disappeared completely. The Provins rose had tangled itself around the arbor seat, and instead of glossy green leaves and sweet-scented blooms, its brown stems bore giant thorns, like those of the Savior's crown.

Plucking at the remains of my fennel, with her back to me, was a stooped old woman. There was something familiar about her movements, and when she turned slightly, I saw the sharp nose and straight mouth and knew that it was not an old woman, but Dame Bewick, strangely altered. She saw me.

"The witch!" cried Bewick hysterically, crossing herself. She reached for the broom plant, snapped off a dry branch, and quickly formed a crude crucifix, which she waved wildly in my direction, expecting me to melt, I suppose, as witches do in front of the true cross.

"You old fool!" I said. "I'm not a witch. Where is Elinor?"

"Wulfstan! Wulfstan!" Bewick screamed wildly, "Lock her up!" Wulfstan, who had been weeding in a far part of the garden, came lumbering toward us. "Why did you return when there is no one here who needs you?" Bewick continued. "It was your work to prevent the Plague and instead you brought it!"

"Where is Elinor?" I asked again as Wulfstan grabbed me roughly by the arm.

"You should know where Elinor is! You were the witch who stole her! But you'll not see her! I will hang fennel on her door to protect her from your evil. I am the Wise Woman of Bedevere now. Lock her in her tower room, Wulfstan!"

"It's not for you to give orders," I said. "Or for you to follow them," I added to Wulfstan. "Where is Lord Robert?"

"Do as you're told, Witch-Child," Wulfstan said. "Lady Bewick gives the orders when Lord Robert isn't here. And you have saved him some trouble. He is out looking for you."

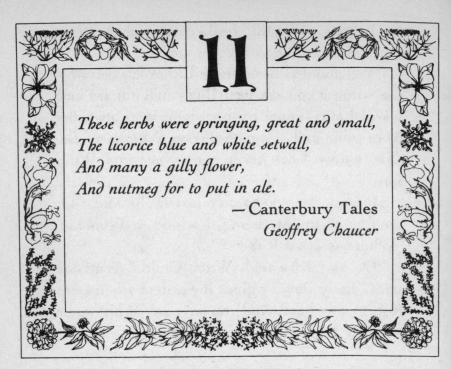

## 11

*These herbs were springing, great and small,*
*The licorice blue and white setwall,*
*And many a gilly flower,*
*And nutmeg for to put in ale.*
　　　　　　　　　　—Canterbury Tales
　　　　　　　　　　　*Geoffrey Chaucer*

"TIE HER UP and do not let her fly away!" Bewick cried, jumping up and down with joy.

"I would not fly away if I could, foolish woman!" I said. "I've come back to see Elinor."

Wulfstan dragged me by the arm over the pebbled walkway of my garden. It was almost covered over with the grass that I had always kept well at bay, plucking it out by the roots whenever the prickly green shoots shoved their way up through the pebbles or the thyme.

"Bring her this way, Wulfstan," Bewick ordered. "You are just in time to be the witch," she said to me. "Only three nights hence when we celebrate the feast of St. John!"

"You don't have to break my arm, you oaf!" I tried to shake off Wulfstan's hairy hand and pretend I was not frightened by Bewick's words. "You've ruined my garden in less than one season!" I said to her. "You didn't take care of the herbs and now they will not take care of you. That fennel is useless. You are not a Wise Woman, and I don't believe you're the Lady of Bedevere, either!"

"Oh yes, I am! I cured Lord Robert when all were stricken by the Plague you brought, and then I cured Elinor from the spell you cast on her. They are grateful to me, and they do not need you. Hurry, Wulfstan, do not let her go!"

I rubbed my arm where Wulfstan's grip had bruised me, and followed Bewick out of the garden, Wulfstan close behind. "I'm not afraid of you, Witch-Child," he said, but he'd let go of me because he was.

Bewick led the way through the castle kitchen, which had the musty smell of disuse and filth. Dirty pots and spoons encrusted with food were everywhere; the fireplace was black and obviously had not been used in weeks.

"Cook and his whole staff were caught by

Pest," said Wulfstan, making the sign of the cross. "I was spared, thanks to Lady Bewick."

I didn't bother to answer; I was too shocked by what I saw.

I remembered a happy day in the larder with Elinor when we had counted the carcasses of twenty oxen and twelve pigs, and seen brined herring by the barrel, as well as nuts, rice, lard, oatmeal, and an abundance of sea salt and spices. Now it stood empty. Mice scurried into dark corners, and dust covered the bare shelves. Only the honey pots were full, and there were a few jars of mead and cider next to two green cheeses and one oaten cake partly nibbled away by mice.

We reached the great hall, where on St. Swithin's Eve the chambers had rung with the sounds of clanging armor, constant chatter, dogs and servants scurrying through freshly scattered herbs and hay, and lords and ladies laughing and dining before the Pest entered and changed everything. Now the place echoed hollowly with the shuffling swish of Bewick's ill-fitting slippers, Wulfstan's heavy wooden shoes, and my own nervous footsteps.

When we reached the spiral steps leading to my turret, Wulfstan shoved me in and slammed the heavy door shut. Before he could throw the bolt that locked the door, I shouted, "Aren't you afraid I'll fly away, Lady Bewick?" I tried to make the word *Lady* sound sarcastic, but tears choked my voice.

There was a silence, and then she said, "You will not fly away, for if you do, you will never see Lord Robert or Elinor."

"I'll not fly away if you promise me I can see Elinor!" I said. They really believed that I was a witch and could fly!

There was another pause while Bewick came up with an answer and it was clever. "I will ask Elinor if she wants to see you," she said finally. She knew that just the hope of seeing Elinor was better than tying me up.

I heard the bolt lock the door. "I will be here if you need me, Witch!" Wulfstan said mockingly.

"You! I will turn you into a bug, and Bewick will squish you by accident!" The silence that followed was gratifying. I had frightened him for now, and he believed with all of his stupid heart that I could do as I said.

I climbed my steps slowly, trying to gather my courage and praying that at least the Monarde was where I'd left it.

The door was slightly open, and through it drifted wisps of the early morning fog that blanketed the castle. My tower was often invisible from the ground, enclosed in a damp curtain of white. I had never minded that. Those were the days when it was too damp to dry the herbs and impossible to search for them in the woods. But with my window shuttered by oiled parchment, my room was more magical than ever, and I could enjoy the warmth from my small brazier and the feeling that in all the world, I belonged just here.

I watched the mist wind its way into the landing from my room, and I knew there was no longer parchment in the window and no hope that my herbs were not moldy and useless from the penetrating damp. I kicked the door open, and a rat scurried along the wall. I waited for my eyes to adjust to the dark. The familiar shape of my oak table was just visible, shoved close to the window. I groped my way to it and touched the smooth surface, sticky with cobwebs and dust. I reached into the small alcove for the Monarde and cut my finger on the broken vessel that had held the three drops of magic. Nothing was left. Bewick must have tried everything, and knowing nothing, she had no doubt hastened the end of many in the castle.

I heard a sound and noticed something alive and white under the steps leading to the roof.

Suddenly there was a great beating of wings, and a large white bird flew past my face and out into the lifting fog. It was the stork that had once nested on the roof. Under the steps there was a round nest with an egg in its center, shining in the dark like a small oval lamp. It was comforting to know there was life in my room.

I watched the stork fly into the rapidly disappearing fog. Nothing seemed changed from this great height: even the stink of the moat managed to rise as high as my nostrils. I could see cattle and crops in the distance.

Looking down the road as far as the forest, I spotted a small cloud of dust, a rider galloping toward me. As he came nearer, I saw that the horse was as white as Lord Robert's Purity. I strained my eyes, and as the horseman came closer I could see that it was Lord Robert.

Even though he had told me that if I came back he would see to it that I was burned as a witch, he was my only hope. I'd have to convince him that Bewick was the witch, not I.

I leaned out the window as far as I could and waved my kerchief. He slowed Purity to a trot; at the drawbridge he halted and stared. His hand, shielding his eyes, hid his expression, but I thought he gave me a nod, and I wondered if his greeting was a welcome or a threat. He rode over the bridge, Purity's hoofs clip-clopping against the wood.

He passed through the gate by Old Henne's hovel, just as he had that first time when I'd saved his life with the foxglove. What harm was there in trying a small spell of magic on Lord Robert? I could catch his eye and say:

> *Robert, Robert, look at me!*
> *A pure heart is what you see!*

Clear as a chapel bell ringing, I heard Gallena, "Tricks are tricks and witchcraft is evil!" Her words restored me to my senses so quickly that by the time I heard the lock clang open, I was Ceridwen, Elinor's companion and the Wise Woman of Bedevere.

He stood at my door, and I curtsied. "M'lord," I said humbly.

"Is it really you? Or be ye a fairy?" he said. "I have searched the countryside for you. Tell me true now, Ceridwen: what are you?"

"I am not a fairy or a witch! I am Ceridwen, the Wise Woman of Bedevere."

"Then can you lift the spell you put on Elinor?" he asked.

"Spell! What's wrong with Elinor? Dame Bewick told me that she had cured her!"

Lord Robert hesitated a minute. He seemed

to be trying to decide if he could trust me, and so I said, "I came back because I promised Lady Isobel I'd take care of Elinor. I came back even though you told me not to because I thought Elinor might need me. Now Bewick has locked me up and says I will be the witch on the hill!" My voice broke. "I'd never cast a spell on Elinor even if I knew how. I told Lady Isobel . . . What ails Elinor?"

He sighed. "I'm not sure. I thought it was the enchantment you put on her in the forest. You covered her with a blue ointment, and she asked me how I could see her, because you'd made her invisible."

"That was only woad to make a small illusion so that we could hide in the shadows!"

"She became very ill the next day. Everyone in the castle had already been stricken by the Plague that you had brought into the castle," he added coldly. "Lady Bewick never came down with it, and she nursed and saved most of us with herbs from the garden. When I returned with Elinor, she saved her, too, and then she announced that she was the Wise Woman and the Lady of Bedevere. Only . . . something . . . something is still wrong with Elinor. I have looked for you everywhere because I know you can cure her."

"How can I cure her when Bewick has had me locked up and . . . and I don't have my book with all of its receipts?"

"You left it when you stole Elinor," he said. "You were in the chapel dressed as Mother Iraine. Lady Bewick found it and used your remedies to cure us."

"Then that is perhaps what ails Elinor," I said angrily. "Dame Bewick knows nothing of the healing arts and no doubt made things worse!" I would never learn to hold my tongue. "I need my book," I could hear the whine in my voice. "And I did not steal Elinor," I added. "I brought her to the convent in order to save her life. I knew Death was in Bedevere."

"You could have told me," he said, changing his tone a little. "You know that."

"There wasn't time," I said.

"Here." He reached into his doublet and brought out a small package wrapped in green cloth. "Lady Bewick gave me your book. She wanted to burn it, but I have kept it with me." His eyes were fixed on me, and I hid my reaction as best I could.

I recognized the green material; it had been cut from the sleeve of the first dress Lord Robert had given me. I wondered why he'd kept my sleeve and carried my book. Was it out of fear that I was a witch and could harm or protect him? Or was it possible that he cared for me? I ventured a quick look at his face and had my answer.

Who knows what might have happened if I'd said, "Together we will save Elinor no matter what ails her!" Instead, I took a timid step backward, a deep breath, and said as usual the wrong words, "Give me my book and take me to see Elinor. I have to see her first. Then I will do my best." Even to my own ears I sounded cold and forbidding.

His light blue eyes turned to ice. "No. Your best may not be good enough. You *shall* save her! I want no mandrake cure. If you fail, then Lady Bewick can decide your fate. Come with me."

Lord Robert led the way to Elinor's room, and I followed. Wulfstan was right behind me. We came to her door, and there she was, standing with her back to us. Bewick was combing her long hair, which had lost some of its sheen, as though the ashes of the midsummer fire had been rubbed into the silver blond tresses.

"Elinor," I said softly. She didn't move. "Elinor?"

She turned slowly, and I heard myself gasp. Her face was hideously altered: her mouth pulled down on one side, her nose fat and flattened, her skin blotched with Plague scars. Worst of all were her eyes. Her eyes were dull and unseeing.

"You're not Elinor!" I cried involuntarily.

"You are a witch, Ceridwen," Elinor said in studied, careful talk. "It is you who invited Pest to Bedevere and stole me from my father. Then you painted me blue with flying ointment and tried to fly off with me, but it didn't work because my father found me."

"It's true! It's true!" Bewick shouted. "The witch-child brought the Plague to Bedevere."

"That is nonsense, and you both know it!" I said. "What have you done with Elinor, Dame Bewick? This creature is a changeling!"

"I am no changeling, Witch! Lady Bewick saved me from the Plague with angelica, and now she is the Lady of Bedevere, and you are the witch."

Lord Robert said nothing and watched me closely. My emotions raced over each other, twisting and turning in confusion. Could this possibly be Elinor saying such things to me? If Pest could twist her face and body into this misshapen creature, could he tangle her thoughts as well?

I turned to Lord Robert. "Gallena taught me that the first thing I must do in order to heal is study and examine. I will have to spend time with Elinor before I know what to do."

"There is nothing for you to know or do!" Bewick screamed. "Go back to your room! Wulfstan! Take the witch-child—"

"Stop!" Robert said. "Lady Bewick, I give the orders and I say that Ceridwen shall have a chance to cure . . . to help Elinor recover. What do you need, Ceridwen?"

"I need only to be with Elinor a while. Let me take her into the woods tomorrow, and together we will gather the herbs and greens for the midsummer feast. But . . . Lord Robert," I said finally, "what if this Elinor that we see here is a fairy's changeling substituted for the true Elinor?"

"Then I believe that you are that fairy," he said angrily, "and you have hidden Elinor and given me another! Do you think that you fool me? You pretend to be only a Wise Woman, but I have always known that you are a sorcerer. If you have stolen Elinor, then you can bring her back. What say you to that?

"Wulfstan," said Robert without taking his eyes off me, "this woman is in your charge. She may search the woods tomorrow with Elinor, but you must see to it that she does not fly away from Bedevere tonight."

Wulfstan looked at me and grinned maliciously.

"For now, take her to her room and stand guard at the foot of the stairs all night," continued Lord Robert. With one more chilling look, he turned and left.

"Fly away now, Witch!" Wulfstan called up to me after he'd brought me to my room.

"Fly yourself, you loathsome toad!" I yelled back.

Unexpectedly, a sob choked me. The stork had returned to her nest and eyed me comfortingly, all but inviting me to share her nest. "Thank you, Lady Stork, I will," I said.

I rolled my gathering apron into a ball and placed it close to the stork's nest. Tomorrow I would put my room in order and take Elinor to the woods to determine if she was the real human Elinor of Bedevere or a changeling.

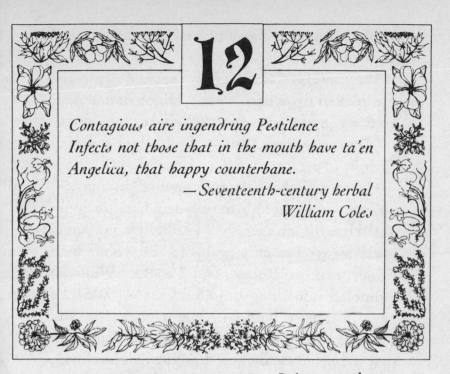

## 12

*Contagious aire ingendring Pestilence*
*Infects not those that in the mouth have ta'en*
*Angelica, that happy counterbane.*
                    *— Seventeenth-century herbal*
                        *William Coles*

AS SOON AS IT WAS LIGHT, I inspected my shelves to see what I could salvage. None of the clay vessels, so carefully formed and baked by the potter especially for my dried and powdered herbs, was left whole. They had been emptied, their contents used or scattered carelessly about, and the vessels shattered.

I dusted the shelves, tore the cobwebs from the corners, and swept my floor, careful not to disturb the white egg in its nest. I washed myself with rainwater that had collected in a depression on the sill and a sliver of herbal soap rescued from the debris.

I tied my gathering apron around my waist and picked up a basket that Elinor had always used when she accompanied me to the woods.

"Open the door, Wulfstan," I called, banging on it.

He turned the key and opened it a crack, peering in as though he expected me to jump out at him. "Don't worry," I said. "I'm not going to fly away; I'm only going to the woods with Elinor, as Lord Robert said I could." Wulfstan mumbled something but stood aside. "We'll be back in time to help with the decorations, and I'll need you to hang the garlands." I thought that if I acted as always, I might win him over.

Elinor was standing by the window, as she had before, with her back turned to me.

"What do you want, Ceridwen?" she asked without turning around.

"How did you know who it was?"

"I have ears. I know your step." She turned, and I tried to control a shudder. She was a hideous parody of her former delicate self. I stared, searching for anything that might identify her as the real Elinor.

"Why are you staring at me? You should recognize your little companion," she said mockingly.

"My little companion was a sweet child," I countered, "and she loved me."

"Not after the mandrake root, she didn't!" She changed her voice, "I want my mother back!" She whined in exactly the way Elinor might have before I convinced her that it did no good to feel sorry for herself.

Was it possible that this child really was Elinor? I asked myself for the hundredth time. This one had duller hair and bigger feet than Elinor's, but young feet grow rapidly, and when you've been sick, hair can lose its sheen. And this Elinor was somehow heavier and clumsy, something Elinor had never been.

I thought that if I could see Elinor's stomach, and if it didn't have a scar from the cut, I'd have my proof.

But even as the thought crossed my mind, I saw a nasty smile on Elinor's face. She had read my thoughts or enough of them to know that I was trying to prove my suspicions.

"I am Elinor," she said. "But I am not sure who you are. Are you Ceridwen, the Wise Woman? Or are you Ceridwen, Witch of Bedevere?" She laughed in a way that told me she wasn't expecting an answer, and I changed the subject.

"Tell me, were you very ill from the Plague?"

"Yes," she said. "If it had not been for Lady Bewick, I would have died."

"What did Dame Bewick do? It takes a Wise Woman to cure, and even she is helpless if the disease goes beyond a certain point. What did Bewick give you?"

Elinor's eyes narrowed. "How would I know? I was unconscious the whole time. And when I first awakened, I didn't recognize my father — and he didn't know me. He thought you'd kept me in the forest with you and given him a fairy child."

"What has changed his mind?"

"I convinced him after a few days. I can remember things," she said shrewdly. "And Lady Bewick told him that you have enchanted us both."

I tried to control my anger. "Elinor," I said as brightly as I dared. "I am going to the woods to gather the garlands and herbs we need for St. John's Eve. Would you care to come?"

I never had to ask Elinor twice in the old days.

"I don't mind," this Elinor answered indifferently.

As we crossed the moat, I remembered how Elinor would skip along, running ahead of me across the mead and into the trees. This sullen child had a lumbering gait and swayed stiffly from side to side, like a fat woman.

When we came to the woods, I slowed my step, waiting to see if the child would take our usual route into the deepest part, away from the path tramped clear by the cattle. But she plodded on and missed pointing out to me the wild thyme, something Elinor would have noticed immediately. When we came to the Rushmore, she seemed as eager to bathe as I could have wished.

"Don't you want to go in?" she asked brightly in Elinor's sweet voice. "I'm hot and weary. Aren't you?" she added as she removed the heavy clogs from her feet.

"I'd love to bathe," I said, taking my shoes off, too, and slipping out of my apron and dress. She was watching me as carefully as I was watching her, and I almost laughed out loud when I realized why. She was hoping to prove I was a witch by the old method: I was supposed to swim or maybe melt in water!

"You go first!" I said.

"No, you!"

She wore a two-piece undergarment, and if

I could lift the chemise just as far as her rib, I would see the place where the scar should be.

"Come," I said, holding out my hand and leading. "We will go together. Oh!" I cried, staring at her midriff as though I'd seen nothing less than a poisonous spider at her waist. "What is that?"

Startled, she pulled up her shirt, revealing her whole stomach, completely unblemished.

"You're not Elinor! You don't have a scar from the cut you got when you fell!" I said with absolute certainty.

"Dame Bewick smoothed it off with pumice!" she answered sweetly.

"You lie! Where is Elinor? What have you done with her?"

The changeling's face contorted, and she spoke in a guttural voice, "He'll never believe you!" Then she changed her voice back into Elinor's. "I am Elinor and I will convince my father that you are a witch!" She picked up her clothes and ran barefoot into the trees, somehow managing to look as light and graceful as Elinor.

"Stop!" I screamed, but she never glanced back. Now I knew positively that the fairies had stolen Elinor and left one of their own, clever enough to mimic Elinor when she chose to.

Hurriedly I gathered mugwort, plantain, corn marigold, dwarf elder, yarrow, ivy, vervain, and orpines needed for the Midsummer Eve garlands and filled my apron pockets with fresh sprigs of St. John's wort for the destiny readings.

I returned to the castle as quickly as I could. It was no use fighting evil spirits with herbs. I needed magic to break this enchantment.

I looked at my book, in which I had written and painted all that I knew. I studied the words, searching for meanings beyond the obvious interpretations. I thought about my past cures, so carefully recorded, and tried to understand why, for example, the herb mugwort reduced trauma in one person while hastening death in another.

I had written down the humors of each patient, characteristics of each that seemed unrelated to the immediate illness at the time. These I reread carefully, and I discovered a relationship. I thought about every scrap of information that I had learned, and gradually, I began to see patterns that combining herbs with certain words and phrases cured illnesses.

Everyone knew that the same words spoken in different tones produces different effects. One can cry "Oh God" in praise and receive comfort, while another "Oh God" spoken in hate calls down a curse from heaven. I made a list of ingredients and a list of words carefully chosen, and I called it Ceridwen's Enchantment. I made a tea brewed from genista, lovage, mistletoe, and comfrey, and said the words:

*Elinor, Elinor! Fly away to me!*
*From the fairies I set you free!*

Elinor's small ghost appeared, thin and wispy with her shining hair and radiant smile, her thin arms stretched out to me. But it was only a ghost. I tried again, adding rue; I came closer to building a solid Elinor, but the ghost was an illusion and had nothing to do with the real Elinor. It was the day before St. John's Eve, and the townspeople were looking for a witch to burn on the hill.

I fell asleep exhausted and dreamed that I was having a long important conversation with Gallena and that I must remember what she was telling me. But when I awakened after a few hours, the only thing I could remember were her words: "Know your name and you will find Elinor."

I tried mixing a potion for changing forms, remembering that the first Ceridwen had been able to accomplish a transformation in the wink of an eye. But I was slow and unable to turn myself into anything other than a Wise Woman who knew a few tricks and illusions.

It was the night of the Midsummer's Eve, the longest day and shortest night of the year. St. John's Eve would be celebrated tomorrow. Time was running out on me.

If Elinor was with the fairies, they would be in the forest, moving about at night. This was my last chance to get her back. Wulfstan had locked the tower door again, but that was not an obstacle. I had a buckle with a prong that could probe inside the keyhole and throw the pawl that moved the bolt. If Wulfstan was sleeping, I could slip past him.

Gently, I pushed the metal prong into the keyhole. I probed left and then right. When I felt the end of the prong firmly set against metal, I pushed as hard as I could to the right. For a moment nothing happened, and then the pawl flipped over with a slight click and the door was open.

Wulfstan was snoring loudly. I slipped out, and a draft of air blew past. He stirred, and I quickly put a pinch of monkshood under his nostrils. He opened one eye, and I said:

*Sleep, you oaf,*
*And I'll slip by.*
*Into the woods I will fly.*

Wulfstan breathed in and lapsed into a deep slumber that I knew would last into the morning.

# 13

*Come away, O, Human child!*
*To the woods and waters wild,*
*With a fairy hand in hand,*
*For the world's more full of weeping*
*than you can understand.*
                    *— "The Stolen Child"*
                    *W. B. Yeats*

DEEP IN THE FOREST, the full moon changed its light into ribbons that dotted the earth with silver coins. Suddenly I saw a circle of tiny lights, and there in the middle stood Elinor! Her moonbeam hair shone as she swayed to the tinkle of fairy music. The fairies were dancing around her, singing an old song and weaving olden dances, mingling hands and mingling glances.

If Elinor saw me, she would cry out, and the fairies would spirit her away to where I could not follow. I froze like a nocturnal animal whose presence is given away only by eyes that glow in the dark. I had the ingredients for the enchantment, but the words would not come out right. I took a chance, and with little hope, I said aloud:

*Elinor! Elinor! Come back to me!*
*Make the fairies set you free!*

In a twinkling, the fairies disappeared, taking Elinor with them. Was it the vision of a second or an all-night trance? I would never know, for time and place are enchanted in the fairy world. When the early dawn erased the moonbeams, I had not brought Elinor back, and I found myself on the banks of the Rushmore at the very spot where I had once washed the soot from Elinor's hair.

What good was my proof that there was a changeling at Bedevere if the fairies still had Elinor? I could not convince anyone simply by telling them what I'd seen. I had heard of one way to prove that a child is a changeling: Lay it on the fire and chant, "Burn, burn, burn — if of the Devil, burn, but if of God and the saints, be safe from harm!" Then, if it was a changeling, it would rush up the chimney with a cry, but if it was human, it would be unharmed. But I believe that fire will burn both phantom and human, and I did not want to use this test on the changeling for fear that even a tiny part of her might be human.

The evil spirits would be gathering on Midsummer Eve. Some call it Witches' Night, although it is the eve of the birthday of St. John the Baptist and good Christians make the fires on the hill in the saint's honor. But in their hearts, it is really the pagan god Baal that the people fear, and they whisper prayers to him, hoping to appease him by burning an effigy as well as honor the saint. I did not want to take the place of that effigy.

As I crossed the courtyard, I glanced up and saw the changeling watching me from her window. I had no doubt that she was encouraging Lord Robert's distrust of me. But at times he must have remembered the tranquil days he'd spent in my garden, sitting in the arbor, thinking comfortably out loud as I puttered around the herbs with Elinor. And, of course, he must have sometimes reminded himself that I had brought him back from the dead. Maybe it was for the sake of the past that he had told me to make the Midsummer Eve preparations as I always had. Yet when he said it, I saw suspicion and speculation in equal proportions written on his face.

I had worked at fleshing out Elinor's small

ghost, which still appeared unsubstantial, and I'd even considered showing Robert how close I had come to bringing Elinor back, but I was afraid he would know it was only a trick.

I climbed the steep stairs to the landing by my door. Wulfstan was gone, but I heard voices coming from my room. I froze and heard Bewick say, "I have seen her at her mischief! Disguising herself as a large white bird she was, in this very room! First she annointed her body with blue flying ointment. I saw it through the keyhole, I tell you! Her bare white limbs grew feathers and soft down sprouted around her breast! Then her neck lengthened like a stork's, and large feathers sprang from her arms like sleeves. She hopped to the window and flew away over the castle wall to the village! And that very day, Robert, when Old Henne fetched the cattle in, Agnes Thorpe's firstborn girl was stricken with a fit while watching a flying stork!"

"But I myself was with her that day!" said Robert, and then, perhaps embarassed at the possible interpretation of his remark, he added, "That is, I saw her about the castle in the afternoon, and she was busy treating the miller's wife."

"You watch her closely," Bewick said. "Are

you not sometimes suspicious of her activities?"

"Anyone with the healing arts has ways strange to ordinary people. I do not believe she is a witch."

"But I tell you she is! I saw her change her form. And look at this nest and egg! What do you say to that?"

"I say that you should spend more time with Elinor and less spying on Ceridwen!" said Robert angrily. "You brought me up here, but we have found nothing incriminating except these feathers and a nest, which could belong to any stork. Ceridwen is our only hope to cure Elinor. Don't you realize that?"

"What I realize," retorted Bewick as angry as he, "is that you are blind to the truth! Blind with love for a witch! There is nothing wrong with Elinor that time will not cure, and if you were not enchanted, you would see that the writing in Ceridwen's book is done with dried blood and is the handwriting of the Devil! And that bird's nest is her bed! At this very moment she may fly in the window! She has cast a spell on you —"

"Go to your room," Lord Robert said in a deadly voice. "If you are wrong about Ceridwen, I will see that you end your days at St.

Agatha's with a vow of silence to seal your lips!"

Bewick did not answer, and I heard the angry rustle of her silks just in time to flatten myself behind the door as she hurried down the stone steps. I waited to hear Robert follow, but I heard nothing more. When he didn't leave, I peered cautiously through the crack in the door and saw him standing motionless by my window, staring at a white feather in his hand.

If only I had remained hidden and left him to work out his thoughts, things might have turned out differently, but I stepped into the room.

"Robert!" I said. Even to my ears it sounded too intimate.

He looked up, surprised but unguarded for only a second. "How did you get into the room?" he asked coldly.

I laughed. "Surely you don't think I flew in with stork wings?"

He didn't smile. "Tell me truly, Ceridwen," he said sternly, "in the name of our mutual love for Elinor, have you cast a spell on me?"

I was so astonished by his words that I answered lightly, trying to hide how deeply they had touched me. "And do you also believe, like

Bewick, that I enter this turret room on stork wings?"

His tone changed again, to match mine. "I do not care how you travel about. You can come and go as you please, and I have no doubt that you have the power to turn yourself into anything you choose. I am only interested in what you have done with my daughter. Ceridwen, you have gone beyond the time I allowed, and I can no longer protect you." So saying, he brushed past me and was gone.

I went through the rest of the banquet preparations in a kind of daze. I had lost my one chance to win him over. I went over the scene a hundred times, thinking each time of a better way to have answered, a way that would have kept him from turning against me. Why did I never say the right words when I needed them most?

I worked without thinking of what I was doing. I wove tiny golden shoots into wreaths of birch, and I fashioned candles into small boats of wood to set adrift at night on the moat. I found an old apron for the straw witch and made a broom for her out of dried genista branches. I went to the kitchen and inspected the pastry dragon made by the baker, which Wulfstan, dressed as St. George, would "slay" after the feast.

Then I returned to my room, dressed in a gown Lady Isobel had given me in my early days at the castle, and went out through the inner courts and across the bridge. Old Henne was not in her accustomed place, having already joined the villagers on the mead. There were more people than I had expected; they had come from far and wide and seemed as large a crowd as ever in spite of what the Plague had done to their numbers — one from every three, it was said.

The midday feast was spread out on trestle tables for all and sundry. I avoided Robert, who stood quietly with the changeling at his side, but he strode across the lawn and invited me to sit next to him at the banquet.

I was flattered and took his kindness as an apology for the way he'd acted before. After we were seated and the tankard was passed to me, I did not notice that my goblet of May wine smelled heavily of monkshood, nor did I see that Robert watched me drink with more than pass-ing interest. The sweet feeling of well-being turned rapidly into thick stupefying drowsiness, and by the time I realized that I'd been drugged, I was already bound. My hands were tied behind me, and a piece of linen around my head covered my mouth. I was being carried somewhere and I was conscious that time was passing, but I did not know how much.

# 14

Green is gold,
Fire is wet,
Future's told,
Dragon's met.
—*Midsummer's Eve riddle*

"GET UP, WITCH," Wulfstan said, his foot in my ribs. I was on the dungeon floor. Wulfstan was still dressed as St. George. "Your trial begins!" he added dramatically.

He pulled me to a standing position and shoved me up the steps to the blinding light of the upper castle rooms. I was led into the great hall, where a motley group was clustered in a corner. Lord Robert, with Bewick on his right and the dreadfully smiling changeling on his left, sat at a table facing the serfs and villeins of the castle. I was shoved before the table, in front of Lord Robert.

"You are charged with witchcraft," he said without any feeling, "with bringing the Black Death to Bedevere, and with stealing Lady Elinor. Defend yourself!"

I prayed but not only to God. "Gallena," I cried silently, "Come to my aid!" I felt my head clear and began to speak.

"I swear by the Holy Cross that I have never practised witchcraft," I said. "I did not bring the Plague nor did I steal Elinor or do any of the things you accuse me of. It was not I who soured Farmer John's cream or gave Dame Edythe the itchy rash. It was Dame Bewick, who wants to be your great lady, who meddled in my herbs without knowing the healing arts. . . ."

I got no further. Everyone started shouting, "She blames others to take the blame from herself! Burn the witch before she does us more harm!"

I stood before them, dressed in the old rags of Mary of the Moat. My hair was knotted and matted with the filth of the dungeon floor, and my hands were tied behind my back. I looked the part of Ceridwen, Witch of Bedevere.

I tried to continue. "I have no knowledge of how to rid Elinor's body of its present occupant." They began to cry out against me again. Bewick could not sit still. It didn't matter what I might say in my defense — she had already found me guilty, and the rest wanted a witch to burn. What chance did I have?

I looked at Robert, but I couldn't read his expression.

"If I were a witch, don't you think I would turn myself into a great bird, as Dame Bewick claims she has seen me do? Don't you think I would flap my wide wings and fly far from here to escape the flames you will light for me on the hill?"

I could not contain a sob as I looked around the great hall for a sympathetic face. There was not one in the lot. All of those who had once implored my help and showered me with gifts, kissed my hands, and praised and honored me now looked eager to dance over my ashes.

"I know that you will never believe me, and that I stand condemned as well as accused. Still I say, for the sake of the true Elinor, that someone ignorant of herb knowledge meddled with my herbs, and Elinor's plight is the result of experiments made by one of my accusers!"

There was shouting: I could make out, "She

lies!" "She shifts the blame to us!" and "She caused this mischief!"

"I saw you do all of it! I saw you do it!" shrieked Bewick, bobbing up and down with excitement. "You made a little doll just like my little lady Elinor, and you stuck a pin in its head! And all the while you chanted a spell. I heard you! I saw you in your tower! And in that very moment, Elinor cried, 'My head hurts!' and — may God have mercy on her soul — came down with the sickness and changed before my eyes! The witch Ceridwen did it, I tell all of you!"

"Wait! Wait!" shouted a familiar voice. There stood Old Henne, smiling her toothless grin and looking at me with affection. "You people you, what's this!" she cried to the increasingly large group gathered in the great hall. "The waif a witch! Have you lost your senses? You should know better — the many times she's cured you with her herbs! Why look at me — 'tis her and her herbs has seen me through."

I had always had a fondness for Old Henne, who'd taken care of me when no one else would, and here she was coming to my defense once more.

"I'm glad of that, Ma Henne," I said fervently, "but which herb saved you?"

"Why, lass, all of 'em and none of 'em!" Old

Henne chuckled at her own cleverness. "I saw the lad that carried the sickness over the moat, and I said to myself, 'tis the Black Death himself a crossin' my bridge, and it's Waif'll know the cure! But by the time I got my old bones up the steps to your room in the clouds, days had passed and there was pestilence everywhere and you'd gone. So I just helped myself to a pinch of this and a peck of that and was gathering my skirts to make the long climb down them steps — I considered dropping from the window to the moat, I did, so long a way it was, but I can't swim." Old Henne paused to chuckle. She cast a baleful eye on the changeling and seemed to notice her for the first time. There was a long silence while they stared at each other, Elinor still smiling in an awful way.

"What did you do then, Dame Henne?" I asked, hoping to encourage her.

"Why I hid," she said. "I heard footsteps, and along came Dame Bewick, that one there," she said, pointing to Bewick, "dressed like a peacock with the face of a hatchet." I heard laughter and saw fury written on Bewick's face. "She had your book, she did, and I thought that meant you were dead, but bless you and me, too, girl, here you are, live and lively and pretty as ever!"

"What did the dame do?" It was not easy keeping Old Henne on the subject.

"Why, she studied the herbs, she did. She checked each one, opening this, smelling that, reading the writing you'd put on so nice and consulting the book again. Then she swore and swept the whole lot of vials to the floor and stomped on them in a regular rage and turned on her heel. There was not a whole vessel left — save one."

"One was left? Which one?" I held my breath for her answer.

" 'Twas one hid in a dark corner. She'd a smashed that, too, if she'd noticed it. But she didn't."

"Did you take it then?"

"I was about to when I heard the pitter pat of little feet, and I hid again. That one took it!" Old Henne shouted suddenly, pointing a bony finger at Elinor.

"You lie!" screamed Elinor in an ugly guttural voice.

"Nay, Nay! I saw ya! Ya held three pearly drops in your little hand, and then you swallowed them and fell down dead. I saw ya! You was dead!" Old Henne crossed herself, surely the first time I'd ever seen her do that. "You *are* dead!"

"Stop!" I screamed as the changeling charged across the great hall after Old Henne. But Old Henne was still quick for her years, and she fled so quickly that the changeling turned back.

"Burn the witch!" the changeling cried in Elinor's voice.

"Burn the witch!" shrieked Bewick.

It didn't matter what I had said nor that Old Henne's tale had the ring of truth. Bewick continued to shout hysterically, gathering to herself the passion for violence in the others.

"Yes! Yes!" they shouted.

"Guilty!" screamed Bewick, crazy with joy.

*Burn the witch!*" they all shouted.

Robert stood slowly. In his hands he held my book.

"Robert!" I cried. "Believe in me, and we'll bring Elinor back!"

He looked directly into my eyes, his anguished face at last and too late showing the feeling that his words belied: "I find you guilty!" he said.

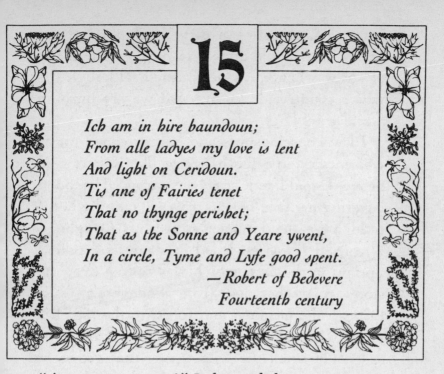

# 15

*Ich am in hire baundoun;*
*From alle ladyes my love is lent*
*And light on Ceridoun.*
*Tis ane of Fairies tenet*
*That no thynge perishet;*
*That as the Sonne and Yeare ywent,*
*In a circle, Tyme and Lyfe good spent.*
                    *— Robert of Bedevere*
                    *Fourteenth century*

"I'M NOT A WITCH!" I shouted, but no one was listening.

Wulfstan yanked the rope that bound my hands behind my back and dragged me out of the hall and into the inner bailey, where a cart such as the one used to transport harvested grain stood waiting.

Bewick was directing everything; she shoved a cup in my face. "Drink this!" she said. It smelled of vervain, and when I turned my head away, Wulfstan poured some of the repulsive stuff down my throat. "Now the mouth," Bewick said, adjusting a dirty cloth around my head. "She should appear to be a woman made of straw when we have finished, although the whole countryside knows that we are burning a real witch!"

I lost consciousness and half dreamed that I was encased in a suit of armor like Robert's, so heavy I could not move my arms. The hood covering my face had narrow slits, and when I tried to breathe, I inhaled straw dust. Coughing, I realized I was enclosed in straw and bound upright in the cart, which was rolling over the stony road that led from Bedevere's walls through the meadow and forest to the hills beyond, where the bonfire was ready to burn.

I could smell the wild thyme that grows in the rutted ways as it was crunched by the hooves of the oxen and the wheels of the cart. I could not move or speak, and I could barely see or breathe. I tried to control my panic, but it was no good. I prayed again, this time to God and his saints, "Lord and St. Swithin, guard me from the flames!"

I heard an answer, but it was Gallena's voice, "Ceridwen!"

The thought of my name mocked me — Ceridwen the Sorcerer! Once, at the beginning of time, I had known the secrets of sorcery, but that was too long ago, and I had forgotten how to do magic. I had searched my mind for the ingredients of Ceridwen's cauldron and the incantations that went with that brew, but now when I needed magic, I could not even think of the first word.

When Gwion stole his three drops and became a sorcerer, he had escaped with some of my wisdom. I remembered how I had pursued him in his changing forms, how I had devised each time a cleverer disguise and changed my form until as a hen I ate the grain that was Gwion. But the names of the right herbs and the magical incantations were lost in time. I was going to burn.

I groaned thinking of it. "Gallena!" I called, but only "Ceridwen!" echoed back to my mind.

I myself had selected the young birch tree to which the effigy would be tied, and I had helped gather wood for the fire and straw to form the witch; I had donated a worn-out apron in which to clothe her. Now I could see a corner of it out of the slit near my eye: the yellow color of broom weed encircled the waist of the straw woman that was myself.

I had thought that the witch looked realistic.

She would be pleasing to the old gods as well as the new One, and her ashes would make rich fertilizer for the crops.

The summer had been dry, and the straw wrapped around me would crackle and ignite quickly. *No!* No, I thought, I won't give up. Think. The potion Bewick had given me was beginning to wear off, and the fuzzy ends of my thoughts were sharper and starting to connect with ideas.

Help from the outside was impossible. The one person who might have saved me had turned against me. I heard his voice shout an order, "Faster, you fool!"

Through the straw I caught a glimpse of his hair, glossy as flax in the sunlight, and I heard Purity's shoes clopping along the hard dirt road, the crack of the whip as the driver smacked the backsides of the oxen and the cart jerked forward at a clip. I could smell the dust as it rose from the road and heard the animals snort, trying to clear their nostrils.

They say that just before you drown, your entire life passes before your mind's eye in a matter of seconds. Now, as I rolled through the clouds of dust into the cool forest to my death on the hilltop, vivid, unrelated scenes appeared behind my eyes: I was kneeling on the cobblestones, slipping foxglove under Robert's tongue; I saw again the Plague-ridden serf dance his way into the hall; and I saw Elinor's face break into a mischievous smile and heard her merry laughter as I did an imitation of Bewick scolding.

I saw Gallena leaving me and handing me the Monarde that I had forgotten and left behind when I fled Bedevere with Elinor. To be used only once in desperate circumstances, Gallena had said, and in my desperate moment, I did not have it. The price of life is death — what did the riddle mean? What would happen if I could take the Monarde now? Suddenly I knew — I understood what Old Henne had seen!

I had been too upset at my trial to understand, but now it was clear. When Robert and Elinor had galloped away, leaving me in the forest, I had heard a sneeze and knew that the Black Death was riding with them. Elinor had known it, too, and she had taken the three drops of magic because I had told her about it. The fairies, who must always have wanted her, had given her life in place of the Black Death, but they had taken her with them and left the changeling in her place. Old Henne had seen it all happen but had not understood what she was seeing.

The wheels left the soft earth of the forest, and I felt the wagon tilt as the oxen inched their way up the hard side of the hill. Once again the dust rose from the path, enveloping the wagon, sifting through the straw, coating my eyelashes, and clinging to the fine hairs that lined my nostrils.

I heard a muffled cough close by my ear and saw the blade of a knife. At first I thought someone was going to stab me, a merciful end to spare me from the flames, but then I realized the thongs that bound the effigy were being cut so that I could be lifted out and placed on what would be my funeral pyre.

Out of a corner of the distant past or perhaps the yet-to-arrive future, I heard my name spoken again. It might have been a memory, or maybe it belonged with a prophecy, but it was then that I understood my name in the old sense: my sorcery did not come from herbs in a cauldron or from three drops of magic, but from knowledge and faith in who I was. I was Ceridwen, with all of the gifts that belonged to that name, and just as I had used my magic and changed my form to pursue the thief of my child's wisdom in that long-ago time, so must I do it again, for Elinor and for myself.

I saw the changeling clumsily jumping for joy.

I heard her shout, "Burn the witch! Burn Ceridwen!" in her ugly voice, just the opposite of Elinor's. I saw Robert staring at her in amazement and horror. Too late, he was seeing his mistake. How could she ever have fooled him? In her excitement, she had forgotten to mimic Elinor, and now, Robert saw her for what she was.

The cart rolled slowly up to the top of the hill, where the frenzied people sang and danced. Robert was running to the wagon. Was he going to try to save me after all? It was impossible to tell, because Wulfstan got there first and lifted me high over his head in triumph. Some of the other men helped carry me to the platform, and Bewick rushed up to be the first to kindle the dry twigs. Robert was shaking the changeling and yelling something I could not hear above the crowd shouting, "Burn the witch! Burn the witch!"

With all my heart and the deepest power within me, I willed the changeling back to the fairy woods and called out loud:

*Elinor! Elinor! Come back to me!*
*I am Ceridwen and I set you free!*

I saw the changeling begin to shake her head. "No, no!" she cried. She seemed to be shrinking, growing thinner. Her struggling, awkward movements gave way to Elinor's grace, and just as the flames ignited the straw of my dress, I heard the changeling cry out as though the flames had scorched her. I heard Elinor cry, "Father! Stop them!" I was watching Elinor take possession of her own form. She threw her slim body against Robert and cried, "Cerri's not a witch! Don't let them hurt Cerri! Stop them!"

I had done it! I had brought Elinor back with my magic, which was stronger than the fairies' because I was Ceridwen the Sorcerer. Quickly, in my newfound wisdom, I chose another form.

> *Small, small, I must shrink*
> *Into a bird, quick as a wink.*
> *Arm change to wing!*
> *Feathers cling!*
> *Fire keep at bay,*
> *Now fly away!*

In an instant, my limbs grew shorter and my arms grew stronger; I lost the power of speech and gained the power of flight. I became a small white bird, small enough to squeeze between the stiff burning straw of my encasement and flutter up to the top of an oak.

From the tree I could see Robert standing

apart, still and unbending, and Elinor jumping up and down, clapping her hands in delight. "She did it, Father! I saw her! She turned herself into a bird and flew away!" Elinor spun around to Bewick. "You only burned the straw witch, you big toad! Cerri found her hidden power and she escaped."

Bewick stood with her mouth open, staring at the real Elinor, as Robert lifted her to his saddle and swung himself up behind her.

The straw witch burst into orange flame, and as she fell apart I watched the dancers shout and leap for joy. When the fire burned lower, they jumped over the embers singing, "The witch is dead, Mother Granno!"

I watched the children light the torches and carry them, dancing like fireflies through the moonless night, over the field sown with rye. They held the torches high, singing, "Granno, my friend, Granno, my mother!" shaking the ashes to the ground so that the grain might grow and the trees bear fruit. Into the barns they skipped, singing, "Granno, our mother, we offer you our gifts! Let the hens lay and the cows give milk!"

When the people had made their way home, exhausted from their spent hate, I flew back to my turret window, and for one last time I stood there as Ceridwen, the Wise Woman of Bedevere.

Just as Lord Robert and Elinor crossed the moat on Purity's back, Elinor looked up and saw me in the moonlight. "Look, Father!" she cried. "It's Cerri!"

Robert looked up, and I waved. Then, as easily as slipping into a new dress, I became a stork and flew away into the night.